HARBINGER
GUARDIAN SECURITY SHADOW WORLD

KRIS MICHAELS

Copyright © 2024 by Kris Michaels

All rights reserved.

No part of this book may be reproduced in any form or by any electronic or mechanical means, including information storage and retrieval systems, without written permission from the author, except for the use of brief quotations in a book review.

❦ Created with Vellum

GUARDIAN SECURITY SHADOW WORLD

CHARACTER LIST BOOK 13 - HARBINGER

Book	Character Name	Spouse	Child (c)
1	(1) Anubis "Ani" / Kaeden Lang (s)(h)(p)	Sky Meyers Lang (w)(p)	Kadey Meyers Lang
2	Asp / Isaac Cooper a/k/a "Mac"	Lyric Gadson	
3	Lycos / Ryan Wolf (h)(p)	Bethanie Clark Wolf (s)(w)(p)	Ethan Simmons Wolf (s*)(a)
4	Thanatos / Dolan McDade (h)	Eve Salutem McDade (w)	
5	Tempest / Luke Wagner (h)	(2) Pilar Grantham Wagner a/k/a Karina Annika Petrov (s**)(w)	
6	(1) Smoke / Dan Collins (s)(h)	(4) Charlotte "Charley" Jacqueline Xavier Collins (s)(w)	
7	Reaper / Roman Alexander (h)(p)	Harmony Flinn Alexander (w)(p)	(1) Iris
			(2) Carter
8	Phoenix / Shane Walsh [e]	Aspen Kennedy a/k/a Nicola Rossi [e]	
9	Valkyrie [W](w)	(1) Smith / Smithson Dimitri Young (s)(h)	
10	(1) Flack / Troy Masters (s)(t)(h)(p)	(1) Addison "Addy" Jean Wilson Masters (s)(w)(p)	Brooke Shankle Masters (a)**
11	(1) Ice / Zack (s)[h)	(1) Londyn Chatsworth (s)[W](w)	
12	Malice / alias Mel Adams (h)	Anya Baranov Adams (w)	
13	Harbinger / Heath Morris (s)[e] (real name Horatio Langdon, the Seventh)	(1) Ysabel Archambeau (s)[e]	

Legend

| (#) age order | (s) sibling | (h) husband | (w) wife | (p) parent | (c) child | (t) twin | (a) adopted | (d) deceased | (e) engaged | [W] Widow(er) |

(s*) Ethan is Dixon and Drake Simmons Marshall's biological half-brother. Ethan's mom, Bethanie, is now married to Lycos who adopted him. The 3 brothers meet for the first time in KG Book 13 - Passages.
Dixon and Drake were adopted by Frank and Amanda-King Marshall in Passages.

(s**) Pilar is Tatyanna "Taty" Petrov White Cloud's long-lost sister (from Kings of Guardian).

(a)** Brooke is Flack's niece (her parents are deceased). He and Addy legally adopt her after their wedding.

CHAPTER 1

 *wo years ago:*

HARBINGER LISTENED to the sounds of the Orchestre de Paris warming up as he took his place inside the Philharmonie de Paris. The grand hall surrounding him was an architectural masterpiece. The walls curved and flowed in a beautiful design of function and mastery designed to carry each note, lifting it in perfect harmony. Wooden panels with sound baffles lined the interior. The luxurious seats curved around the orchestra, ensuring each of the nine hundred and twenty-seven attendees felt the vibrations of the performance. The house lights were subdued, with soft glows focusing the eye on the musicians and their instruments. Despite the grand scale, the overall feeling was intimate. Blending into the crowd, Harbinger focused on the task ahead, the music an enjoyable backdrop to his mission. As the orchestra's tune shifted from practice to performance, the audience hushed in anticipation, completely unaware of Harbinger's mission.

Harbinger sat directly behind Guillaume D'Aureville, his target. The crimes the man had committed were too many and too gruesome to list in front of any normal human. The inherited golden hue that hung over the man had kept him out of prison, and his public relations team had done their job well. He was loved for his philanthropic work and lauded as a man of honor; yet the Council knew the truth, and they had convicted him when the courts couldn't or wouldn't. Money and power provided a temporary shield from his heinous crimes against humanity, but there was a force for good at work in this world, and tonight, it would perform its expungement of monsters while concealed in the shadows.

Harbinger's eye was drawn to the first chair violinist. Her long black hair was pulled to the side as she played. Her face was a study of relaxed concentration. It was an expression he knew. The skill and intensity needed to perform at her level became second nature. The expression came from the knowledge you were the best at what you did. It was the same one he wore.

Enthralled with the precision of the woman's skill, the wait for the intermission seemed to pass in mere minutes. Harbinger rose when everyone else did. He followed D'Aureville and his procession to the lounge where the elite gathered. Harbinger waited for his opportunity, then moved. D'Aureville turned to the doors when the chimes rang, colliding with Harbinger, spilling both his and Harbinger's drinks. Harbinger stepped back and lifted his hands, seemingly as an accident. Exaggerating a slur and stagger, Harbinger pushed D'Aureville's hands into the wet mess. He stumbled into D'Aureville a bit more, making sure the man's skin touched the toxin Harbinger had thrown on him.

In French, D'Aureville swore, and his hands swiped at the liquid Harbinger had spilled. "Idiot," the man grumbled, swiping again and again at the liquid with his bare hand. One of his party offered him a handkerchief, but the man waved it away with a curt, "I'm fine." D'Aureville removed his own handkerchief and swiped at his saturated coat.

Harbinger bowed slightly, apologized in a German accent, and removed himself from the area. D'Aureville had enough toxin on his hands to kill him, and the air would soon nullify the toxin on his clothes. Time was now the only necessary ingredient. Making his way to the bathroom, Harbinger rinsed out his glass with hot water and washed his thinly plastic-coated hands as a precaution, even though he was certain none of the drink had spilled on him. He dropped the glass in the trash and walked out into an almost empty lounge. The music from the symphony started as he walked out of the building. He wandered through the park adjacent to the concert hall. Past the first camera, he turned right and ambled behind a large shrub. From there, he made a ninety-degree turn and headed away from the camera-laced area. At the edge of the park, he walked to a motorcycle that had been prepositioned and put on his helmet. There were no cameras there. Harbinger removed his tux jacket, tucked it in the saddlebag, and put on a leather jacket and gloves before getting on the bike.

He rode aimlessly through the city, ensuring he

wasn't followed, before driving into one of the underground parking areas in the 12th Arrondissement. Harbinger parked in the only area where the cameras were out. He was sure they were out because he'd disabled them earlier. Glancing at the hanging wires before taking off his helmet to confirm some eager public servant hadn't fixed the broken camera, Harbinger began the process of becoming himself.

He took off the curly brown wig. The wooly brown eyebrows went next, followed by the large mole that looked more like a boil he'd used to draw attention away from his chin and nose. The adhesive that held them on his face rolled off in a sheet when his gloves rubbed against it. He slipped the false teeth out of his mouth and placed them in a small box he pulled from his coat pocket. Slipping out of his shoes, he stepped onto the concrete, three inches shorter than he'd been at the symphony hall. He opened the car parked next to where he'd maneuvered the motorcycle, slipped on another pair of shoes and a different jacket, and pulled out a messenger bag. Placing the evidence of his transformation into the parked car's trunk, he shut it and locked it. Only then did he take off his gloves and place them in his messenger bag.

The plastic coating over his hands was easily removed and dropped on the concrete as he moved along the line of cars. He walked out of the parking area and headed to the Metro. Palming the phone that had remained in his messenger bag, he sent the text noting his mission had been accomplished. A response hit his phone seconds later.

>>Awaiting validation. Ambulance called to the scene three minutes ago.

Harbinger looked at his watch. A bit quicker than anticipated, but perhaps the bastard had preexisting conditions that helped the toxin work quicker. The decision to use the poison to make the death appear to be a heart attack wasn't his. He'd just as easily use a garrot to sever the man's head from his body, but the powers that be were the ones who determined what message, if any, to send. Sometimes, monsters just needed to be gone without any grand warning. It was one of those times.

Harbinger entered the metro and sat down. He closed his eyes and pictured the spectacular woman seated as first chair violinist. He'd like to meet her. He smiled to himself. Why not? He loved France, classical music, and beautiful women, and he wouldn't be called for a mission for quite some time. Perhaps it was time to delve into the finer things in life.

One year ago:

Harbinger strolled through the darkened streets of Paris. This section of the city was notorious for crime. Not the crime he'd just committed, of course, but small-time heists, random beatings, or a murder or two. The local gangs owned the territory because it was of no use to the Mafia. He'd just staged the body of his last target in a car about two blocks away. With no cameras or witnesses, the death looked like so many others found in the area. Robbed, killed, and left for the police force to find when the city woke in the morning.

Harbinger dumped the gloves that were covered with gunpowder residue in a dumpster a block back. In another alley where he now stood, he deposited the rest of his disguise in another dumpster. As he quietly closed the metal door, he heard the sound of a pitiful cry and then male laughter. The skin on his arms lifted in gooseflesh. Because of his past, there was no way he'd walk away from that sound. The cry didn't sound human, but then again, humans could sound like animals, too. Heading down the alley, he walked toward the noise. Three men were huddled over something lying in the middle of the alley.

"Do it again." One of the men slapped the other as he spoke. "Make it cry again."

Harbinger wasn't sure what "it" was, but he was damn sure no one would make it cry again.

He walked forward and kicked the man closest to him, launching him sideways. Glancing down, he saw the tiny kitten they'd been torturing. "Fuckers," he growled.

The man across from him reached into his pocket as he sprung up. Harbinger didn't hesitate. He grabbed the man's other arm, yanked it straight, and broke the elbow over his knee. The crack of bone and the man's scream would alert any others in the area. Not that he cared. He spun and kicked the third man's knee hard enough to dislocate the joint and drop him to the cold, wet pavement. Whoever they were, they were amateurs.

The first man, who Harbinger had kicked out of the way, stood up with a small caliber gun in his hand. Harbinger smiled and walked directly at the bastard. The outright look of fear on the man's face told him the asshole wouldn't shoot, and if he did, he'd probably miss. He slapped the gun out of the fucker's hand and slammed his face into a brick wall of the building lining the alleyway. Blood sprayed on the brick, turning it darker. The asshole wailed when his brain caught up with the fact that his nose had been pancaked into nothing but a fleshy hump. Harbinger pulled the guy up by the hair and dragged him over to the kitten. "If you ever hurt an innocent again, you'll die. Find a life. This is your one chance. Do you understand?"

The man cried something behind his cupped hands. Harbinger took it as a yes and threw him to the side. Then he bent down and scooped the tiny animal into one hand. Rising, he stared at each of the bastards. He'd recognize them if he ever saw them again.

Harbinger took the kitten home. It barely moved as he walked several miles before using his app and arranging for a ride. The kitten lay still; although Harbinger could see it was breathing. Every now and then, a small mewl emitted from the dirty puff of fur, but the animal didn't try to move out of his hold.

He stepped out of the ride and entered his apartment building. Ysabel would probably be asleep; although she knew he was "flying" back home from the States that night. A necessary lie to protect her and his identity as a Guardian operative. As his key hit the lock, the door opened. "I was waiting up for you," Ysabel said before noticing the kitten. When she did, she reached for the small bundle and carefully cradled it in her hands. She looked up at him and hissed, "What happened? How did it get hurt?"

"I don't know. I found it and couldn't leave it."

"No! Of course not! Let's take the poor baby into the kitchen." Ysabel ran to the kitchen and turned on the overhead lights.

The kitten's eyes were almost matted shut. Together, they cleaned the animal and wrapped him in a warm hand towel. Ysabel found a bottle with a dropper, and after cleaning it thoroughly, they fed the kitten warmed milk a drop at a time. They huddled over the kitten for about ten minutes, feeding it before it fell asleep.

"He's beautiful." Ysabel carefully pet the golden striped fur. Harbinger had no idea what color the animal was before they carefully washed it looking for injuries. It was skinny and had scratches, but all its limbs seemed to move properly. Its stomach wasn't bloated, so he hoped internal injuries weren't a factor.

Harbinger leaned back and put his arm around Ysabel's shoulder as the kitten slept on her lap. "I'll take him to the clinic in the morning." If it survived. That went unsaid because, damn it, he wanted the animal to survive. It had made it through those fuckers and was still alive. It deserved a chance.

"You're the most wonderful person I know. Rescuing a kitten. Such a soft heart." Ysabel sighed and leaned into him.

Harbinger kissed her temple and closed his eyes. If she only knew. She turned to look at him. "How did your work go?"

"Finished without incident, which is always a good thing." There would never be an incident. He'd been trained by the best, and with his skills, he'd never be identified. "We should go to bed."

"You've had a long week." She frowned and looked back at the door. "Where's your luggage?"

He sighed. He'd bypassed the storage facility where he'd dropped his luggage because his mission was once again in Paris. "The airline said it's still in the U.S. I've given them my address. They'll deliver it when it shows up."

"I don't know how you stay so calm. Another reason I love you as much as I do. You're my hero. What are you going to name him?"

Harbinger looked down at the kitten. Its golden fur was peaked at the top of his head. He patted it down, and it sprung right back up. "How about Spike?"

Ysabel chuckled. "Spike? That'll give him delusions of grandeur, won't it?"

"Maybe, but he's a cat. Don't they think they're better than everyone?"

Ysabel chuckled. "They don't just think it; they act like they know it." She stood and cradled the kitten in her arm. "Come to bed. You're exhausted, and he's asleep." She glanced down at the kitten. "You better make it through the night, Spike. We need a pet."

"We do?" Harbinger asked as he stood up beside her.

"Absolutely." She smiled up at him. "Our first together thing."

Harbinger dropped his arm over her shoulder and walked with her to the bedroom. "Well, not exactly our first together thing." He lifted his eyebrows comically when she glanced questioningly at him.

She blushed and smiled. "You're right."

Harbinger closed the bedroom door after they walked through. "Let's find a warm place for Spike to rest. I want to revisit that first together thing again."

Ysabel's soft laughter floated across the space between them. God, he loved the woman. Soon, when the time was right, he'd tell her what he could about his job, introduce her to his friends, and put a wedding ring on her finger. She was everything he needed. She filled a gaping hole inside him. He'd slowly let her into his heart. Before her it was barren, remote, and lifeless. His was a solitary life, one he volunteered for, but her presence had warmed him. The coldness that surrounded him had thawed, and his view of the world tipped on its axis. There was still good in the world; there was warmth and thoughts of a future. With her, he was complete.

. . .

Present day:

He braced his arms against the tile of his shower and let the hot water soak through to the cold that had gripped him since he'd watched Ice get married this morning. Or rather, yesterday morning. The flight back to Paris was mired in memories of Ysabel. Damn Ice to hell for making him go to the wedding and face the memories he'd been doing a fantastic fucking job of running from. The bastard. Harbinger lifted his head and groaned. It wasn't Ice's fault. He'd done it to himself. All the questions that had no answers had grown into a black hole, and that lack of resolution seemed to suck his every chance of happiness into oblivion.

Don't be pathetic. He used the memory of Ysabel's voice saying that to him as his incentive to leave France. He also used it to beat the fuck out of himself as he spun the same old questions over and over again.

As much as he hated to admit it, Ice was right. He needed to make peace with his past and bury the self-doubt and anger. "Easier said than done," Harbinger told himself as he turned off the water.

He toweled off and pulled on a pair of high-end

sweatpants and a t-shirt that cost more than anyone should pay for a shirt before heading to the kitchen and his wine. He opened the door to the temperature-controlled storage area, selected a stout Mourvèdre from the shelf, and shut the door behind him.

He'd need to order groceries and tell his housekeeper he was back. She was cat sitting Spike and would bring him back home, but all that would wait until he'd had a glass of wine and toasted the end of his best shot at a normal life.

Two solid whacks on his apartment door spun him from the counter as he reacted without thought. His thumb opened the weapons safe on top of the fridge, and he pulled out a forty-five caliber. Harbinger rode the slide back to ensure a bullet was in the chamber before he wrapped his fingers around the grip and deactivated the safety. Quietly and carefully, he made his way to the door.

Another knock sounded. "Heath Morris, I know you're home."

Harbinger's frown scored deeper, and he glanced out the peephole to his door. Ysabel's father? *What the actual fuck?*

Harbinger opened the door, sliding his gun into the back of his sweatpants. It would be his luck the fucker would blow his ass off, but he didn't need anyone seeing the weapon. "What the fuck do you want?" To say he didn't want to see her father was the understatement of this and the past century.

Ysabel's father leaned against the doorjamb. His once lightly salt-and-pepper-colored hair was now almost white. The lines of his face seemed to be etched deeper, and he'd lost a considerable amount of weight. His hair, always neatly combed, flew in every direction, and his eyes were bloodshot. His suit was crumpled, and his tie askew. "You must help me."

Harbinger held the door firmly, blocking the man's entrance into his home, as he lifted an eyebrow. The man had refused to help Harbinger when he was trying to contact Ysabel; as a matter of fact, he'd been one of the biggest blockades in Harbinger's way. The idea he'd help that asshat was funny. Harbinger barked out a laugh and attempted to close the door. "Go fuck yourself."

Pierre's palm hit the door, stopping the forward motion. "He has Ysabel, and he *will* kill her."

Harbinger welcomed the bitter cold rage that filled him as he opened the door and squared up on Ysabel's father. "Who?"

"Abrasha Molchalin." The man said the name as if Harbinger should know who he was. A tinge of recognition flitted through his mind and then settled with knowledge—a Russian oligarch involved in the Switzerland debacle. "Please allow me to come in. I need your help."

Harbinger's mind raced with what he needed to do, who he needed to contact at Guardian, and what information did they have on Molchalin. All that slammed through his mind at the same time as he wondered *if* Ysabel was *truly* in danger. He didn't trust her father. The bastard had stonewalled him when he wanted to talk to Ysabel. Still, he needed answers, so he stepped back and allowed the older man into the apartment. "What do you think I can do for you, Pierre? Go to the police. I'm an American businessman; I have no influence here."

Pierre closed the door and leaned against it. "For once, let us be honest. You aren't a businessman. You work for the government. Maybe not the American government, but you aren't who you say you are."

Harbinger turned and walked into the kitchen. His gun in full view. He put away the automatic and poured two glasses of wine, listening for

Pierre to move away from the door. He didn't. Harbinger exited the kitchen, his emotions and thoughts all over the place. He put the two glasses of wine down and took a deep breath as he sat. With the practiced expertise of hundreds of training missions and over twenty-five kills, he forced his emotions into oblivion. "Sit." He nodded to the chair across from him.

Pierre stumbled to the chair and sat down. He grabbed the wine with a shaky hand and downed the glass in two gulps. He wiped his mouth with the back of his hand and panted, "You aren't a businessman. I had you followed. But you lost every investigator I hired. You were there, and then, you were gone. Your business is a shell company."

Harbinger shrugged. "So are many of yours. Just because I don't disclose my financial documents to you doesn't mean I work for a government. Your investigators were chumps. Clumsy and seen immediately. Ditching them was fun. You're grasping at straws. There's nothing I will do for you. *You* ensured I couldn't contact Ysabel, and *she* explicitly said she didn't want to see me. I don't know this man you speak of. Why would he want to harm her? Why would I get involved?"

Pierre popped off the chair and ran his hands through his hair. "She had to do it! She wanted to protect you! I couldn't care less if this man targeted you, but she loves you. The stupid girl is just like her mother. Once they decide they're in love, nothing will dissuade them." The man paced back and forth and shouted at the floor as he walked. "She isn't my *daughter*! She's my *niece*. My sister and I were protecting her, but Léonie died. Ysabel received a letter while at practice and left for a couple of days. I didn't know, but she went to her mother's funeral. There, she received other documents from her mother. I don't know how, but Abrasha found out that Ysabel was his daughter. I had to hide her to protect her."

"Pierre, sit down. You aren't making sense. Why would her father want to kill her?"

"Because of me."

"You?" Harbinger frowned. "What does Abrasha want with you?"

"He wants me to help him steal billions!" The man raged from across the room. "Léonie was the only reason the bastard stayed away from me. She threatened to leave him if he approached my daughter or me."

Harbinger leaned forward and steepled his

fingers, drawing a deep breath. "Pierre, sit down. I need information, and screaming bits and pieces from across the room isn't helpful."

"Didn't you hear me? He said he'll kill her!" Pierre released a guttural cry. "I love her more than life itself. She's my daughter in every way except for blood."

Harbinger pointed to the chair and waited for the man to move. When he finally collapsed in the seat, tears were streaming down his face.

"Let's start at the beginning."

Pierre looked at him, and his exhaustion pulsed across the space in waves. "Why? You don't work for the government. You can't help."

Harbinger slipped into the skin of the deadly assassin he'd been trained to become, and with the frozen crystalized determination of a man whose woman was in danger, he warned, "I didn't say I couldn't help; I said I wouldn't. There's a difference. I may change my mind, especially if this is another ploy to keep me away from her. But right now, you need to convince me you're not hallucinating or out of your mind and explain why Ysabel is in danger. Now, tell me everything you know."

CHAPTER 2

Harbinger watched as Pierre drew a deep breath and let it out. "Abrasha Molchalin is a Russian oligarch. Very wealthy. Made that way by the fall of the Soviet Union. He's in control of most of the oil refineries in Russia. My sister, Léonie, met him more than thirty years ago when he was amassing his wealth. She was in love with the 'bad boy.'" Pierre shook his head and muttered a string of foul words in French. "He got her pregnant. When she told him, he demanded she abort the baby. Léonie would have none of it and broke off the relationship. She would never harm a baby. It was not in her. Only her bad boy was actually the devil, and he held control over her like I've never seen. Here." He pointed to his head.

"If he'd allowed her to have the baby, I would have never known anything about the man. Léonie would have willingly stayed with him."

Pierre stood up and ran his hands through his hair again. "I sent her to America to stay with friends I'd made when I studied abroad. She had no phone, and computers weren't like they are now. My friend lived in a very rural area. Abrasha couldn't find her. Tracking people thirty-five years ago was different and much more difficult. He knew she was in the States but had no way of finding her there. Léonie delivered Ysabel. I traveled to America and adopted Ysabel. She *is* my daughter. That is legal and binding. Léonie returned to Paris alone, and Abrasha was waiting for her."

"Why did she go back to Abrasha?"

"Because my sister was … I hate to admit this, but she enjoyed the demeaning sex. He treated her as less than a person; she reveled in that control. They had a sick type of love, but for both of them, each other was the only person. She tried to explain how he made her feel, but I could never understand. I still can't."

Harbinger leaned back in his chair. "How is

Abrasha a threat? Why did Ysabel break things off with me?"

Pierre plopped down on the chair again and stared at Harbinger for a long minute. "I did not trust you."

Harbinger lifted a single eyebrow. "No shit."

Pierre rolled his eyes. "Americans. I had you followed as soon as I learned Ysabel was dating you."

"I know. As I told you, it wasn't difficult to play with your goons." Harbinger had made a game of disappearing and then tracking the hapless private investigators. He'd followed one of the first investigators back to his office, broke in that night, and gathered all the information he needed about Pierre Archambeau and the man's intent to have him followed. His work wouldn't allow such oversight, and he wasn't going to allow his lover's father to keep tabs on him. When things became serious with Ysabel, and that happened quickly, Harbinger ensured he kept his work far from his lover and kept her father in the dark.

"What do you do, Heath? Are you a businessman who can disappear into thin air, or are you something more?" Pierre asked as he clasped his trembling hands together. "I pray you are more."

He ignored the question. "How do you know Abrasha has Ysabel?"

Pierre closed his eyes. "I have proof." Pierre pulled out his phone and swiped at the face several times. "Here."

He studied the picture of a severed arm. Clasped in the hand was a phone with a number displayed on the screen. "What am I looking at?"

"The detective I hired to keep tabs on the Russian. This was sent to me the night Ysabel went missing from Corsica."

"Corsica?" Harbinger looked up from the phone. "Why would you send your daughter to the place with the highest murder rate in the nation?"

Pierre lifted his eyes slowly. "Family takes care of family."

Harbinger's eyes narrowed. "So, your removal from le milieu is not as complete as you've portrayed."

Pierre shook his head. "It is. I run a legitimate business, but when I needed to protect her, I contacted the caïd and asked for a favor."

The boss of the French Mafia. Well, Pierre did

have connections in very low places, didn't he? "And that favor?"

"To hide her until Abrasha lost interest or I found a way to make him do so. Only it wasn't Ysabel he wanted. It was me."

Harbinger leaned forward. "So, he doesn't have her?"

"He does. Swipe to the right." Pierre nodded to the phone still clasped in Harbinger's hand. Harbinger thumbed across the screen and winced. A gag pulled Ysabel's mouth back in a contorted slash across her face. There were tears streaming down her cheeks, and her thick black waves of hair were snarled and clumped against her face. There was a bruise on her cheek, and her left eye was blackened. Fury filled his veins as he stared at the woman he loved more than life itself.

"When was this sent to you?"

"Three days ago, via text from an unknown number, just like the first picture. I've been searching for a way to contact you. Ysabel never gave me your cell number. I have contacts in customs. They told me you flew to the United States. I hired investigators there, but without more information on you, it was a waste of money. They could find nothing. When you returned, my contact in customs called me. I came here immediately. Are you more than just a businessman? Can you help me?"

"Whether or not I can help you is yet to be determined." Harbinger ignored the question about what he was and pushed his emotions back, even though it was the hardest thing he'd ever done. His next question would determine what he'd be willing to do. "Why did she break off the engagement?"

Pierre swallowed hard. "*I told her to*. I convinced her a simple businessman wouldn't be able to protect her, keep her safe. I also told her Abrasha would kill you as leverage. I believe he would have killed you or anyone else around her to use her against me."

"Why?"

"Her mother sent documents. According to the letter Ysabel let me read, Léonie had collected a massive amount of information about Abrasha's business. She said the information was in the envelope. Information that could be used to stop him from coming after *me*."

Harbinger leaned back. Ah, that bit of information didn't compute. Pierre had just said he didn't think Abrasha was after *him*. Pierre thought

Abrasha was after *Ysabel*. Things were not adding up. "I thought you said Abrasha was after Ysabel, not you? Which is it?"

"He goes after her to get to me." Pierre ran his hands through his hair. "It doesn't matter the who, we are both in danger and because of the information."

Harbinger narrowed his eyes. Flip and flop. Pierre didn't have his story straight or he was so overridden with worry that he wasn't speaking correctly. "Where is it? The information in the envelope?"

"That's just it. The envelope she showed me didn't have the information. Ysabel said it was sealed, but there was only Ysabel's original birth certificate, plus a letter from Léonie apologizing for giving her up. The letter said all the information was in the envelope and that Abrasha would eventually find out about the data breach. She warned Ysabel to flee. That Abrasha might come after her once he realized she was his."

Harbinger stared stone still and intently at the man across from him. Finally, *finally*, he had verification. He *knew* breaking off the engagement wasn't Ysabel's doing. That gut-deep truth had lived through the months of bullshit excuses and reasons he'd created in his mind.

Harbinger could sense that something was wrong. She wouldn't look at him, her demeanor was guarded. "What's wrong?"

"Dance with me?" she asked him, and he automatically stood up. They fell into the waltz and spun around the ballroom. Her gown floated around his tuxedo. She was absolutely beautiful, but there was something ...

"I wanted you to dance with me because I have to tell you I can't marry you."

Harbinger stopped dancing. "What do you mean?" He held her hand still, but she pulled it free. She took off the engagement ring. "I made a mistake. I don't love you. Please have the grace to not make a scene."

"Make a scene?" Harbinger snapped his mouth shut. "Your father is doing this."

"No, I'm doing this. Take this." She grabbed his hand and placed the ring in his palm. "Don't call, don't come after me. I wasn't seeing the truth about our relationship, but I am now. Goodbye, Heath." She turned to walk away, but he went after her. Two men stepped in front of him.

"We don't want to make a scene, but we will. Let it go for now."

Harbinger glared at the bastard holding his arm. He

could kill him in a heartbeat, but the ballroom floor was not the place. He'd find her, and he'd find out what happened to force her into giving him back her ring.

But he never did. Harbinger pushed back the flood of emotion and memories and focused on what Pierre was telling him. "But instead of asking for this documentation, he kidnapped her?"

"Yes." Pierre ran his hands through his hair yet again.

"And he hasn't asked for the information Léonie gave Ysabel?"

"Correct."

Harbinger dropped that line of questioning. "Have you had any proof of life since this picture?"

"None." Pierre ran his hands through his hair and grabbed it this time, pulling harshly. "Abrasha wants me to acquire thirty-seven billion dollars of cryptocurrency. He's given me three weeks to get the people in place to do what needs to be done."

An oddly exact number, wasn't it? "This crypto will come from your holdings?"

"No, others. People I have never met; the list is long."

"Is this theft possible to do?" Harbinger's mind was racing as he built a mission in his mind because it had become one for him whether Guardian sanctioned it or not.

"Steal the crypto? Yes. It would take a massive effort and experienced computer thieves, but yes. Not all cryptocurrencies are on the public blockchains. Privacy-focused crypto and decentralized finance make it doable without detection *for a time*. But most wealthy people's cryptocurrencies are vaulted and guarded with almost unbreakable safeguards. No one is getting into those vaults, which is what I explained to that bastard. Well, to his messengers."

So, he hadn't talked to Abrasha himself. "And the response?" Harbinger placed Pierre's phone on the table.

"He would provide the fobs that hold the crypto. I am to break the code and deposit the funds via routing numbers he'll send me."

"Do you have the people and the technology to do it?"

"I have the technology but not the right people." Pierre flopped his head back against the chair. "But there's no guarantee the son of a bitch will release her if I do what he says. If I go to the police, she'll be killed. I'm under the thumb, as you say. I've started recruiting people to do the work."

Harbinger narrowed his eyes. "You don't trust me, and I don't trust you, but …"

Pierre's head snapped up. "But?"

"I'll make some calls. I'll need your phone. I want to see if I can trace the number that texted you these."

Pierre nodded readily. "It's yours. What else do you need?"

"Right now, privacy. Go home, Pierre. If you're being watched, he'll know you contacted me. You'll need a plausible explanation."

"You were worried about Ysabel, and I came here to deter you from looking into her status."

Harbinger lifted a brow. *That rationale came quickly, didn't it?* "I'll contact you."

"How? You have my phone."

Standing up, he ordered, "Go home, Pierre."

"You'll help me get her back?"

Harbinger looked at the older man and then looked at the door. "I'll make some calls."

* * *

HARBINGER CLOSED the door behind Pierre and moved to the window. He pulled the drapes back slightly and watched the street. Pierre got into his chauffeur-driven car, and it pulled away from where it had been double parked. *Nothing like making it obvious.* He continued to watch as a man got out of a gray coupe and crossed the street toward his building while the car followed Pierre's vehicle at a distance.

Then he went to the living room and put Pierre's phone into his pocket before heading to the spare bedroom. At the back of the closet, he pushed a panel, slid it up, and placed his palm on the exposed screen. The mechanism whirred and then unlocked. Harbinger went into the secure room and put Pierre's phone into a small Faraday box. If the phone had a listening device or tracker, it wouldn't transmit now. He turned the camera on that monitored his front door and pulled out his secure phone, powering it up. Once it had a signal, he pushed the number one.

"Operator Two-Seven-Four, how may I route your call, Sunset Operative Seventeen?"

"I need to speak to Fury and Anubis."

"Hold, please."

Harbinger rolled his shoulders and turned on the cameras that covered his building and the streets outside. The man who had exited the gray sedan was at the front of his building, casually leaning against the wall by the door, scrolling through his phone.

"Fury online."

"Anubis online."

"The line is secure, and Operator Two-Seven-Four is clear."

"I need some help," Harbinger said without pretext.

"Authenticate messenger," Anubis interrupted him.

"Heralder," he replied immediately.

"What's up?" Fury asked.

"I've just been told Abrasha Molchalin has kidnapped my ex-fiancée." Or fiancée, he wasn't sure.

There was a pregnant pause on the other end of the line. Harbinger pulled the phone away from his ear to ensure he was still connected. "Did you hear me?"

"We did," Fury said. "I'm not sure if we're more shell-shocked over the fuckwad Abrasha showing up on our scope so quickly or that you were engaged and didn't inform us."

"Smoke was aware. He's always known about Ysabel. The engagement lasted just over a week. I was going to tell everyone by bringing her back to the States, but she gave the ring back and told me to stop being pathetic."

"Damn. Harsh." That was Anubis, and yeah, Harbinger agreed with him.

"So …" Fury continued, "what does Abrasha want with her?"

Harbinger flicked his eyes to the camera covering his building before he began to unfold the story Pierre told him.

"Does her father or she know what you are?"

"No. Although the father assumed I worked for the government."

"Why?" Anubis asked.

Harbinger explained his fun at playing around with the private detectives Pierre had put on his tail. "It was amusing at the time."

"Do you love this woman?" Fury asked.

"I do, and if what her father told me is true, she still loves me."

CHAPTER 3

Ysabel Archambeau jumped at the sound of something scurrying in the darkness. The battery-operated lamp she was given was waning, and the sounds around her grew louder. Or perhaps her imagination grew louder. The stench of old earth, stale air, and years of decay no longer registered. She'd been left in this long-forgotten crypt for … She closed her eyes. She wasn't sure how long she'd been there. Food and bottled water came irregularly. The bucket she used for her personal needs was changed when food was delivered.

A cot, a battery-operated light, and a sleeping bag were the only comforts provided. She was in Paris. She knew that because she'd toured the underground catacombs before. However, the ruins she was trapped in weren't preserved like the ones the Paris Musée maintained. No, she was being hidden, and the extent of the catacombs was vast. No one would find her down here.

She curled up on the sleeping bag and stared at the dull light illuminating the limestone walls of her prison. She'd been warned. Her father's contacts in Corsica had told her not to go too far out, to stay within sight of the small mountain village, and to be cautious. But, no, of course, she had to go a bit too far. She rolled her eyes. Her bravado had not only gotten her into this mess but had exacerbated it.

Ysabel wiped a tear. "Stop. You did this to yourself." Her voice bounced off the limestone walls surrounding her. *Stupid. Idiot.* She glanced up at the low ceiling. "Heath, God, I'm so sorry." She shook her head. If she could spin back time, there was so much she'd do differently. Words she'd never utter, decisions she'd never make, actions she would never take, but alas, she couldn't go back, and from where she huddled, it seemed going forward wouldn't be an option for long.

That damn envelope. Ysabel looked at the ring on her finger. It belonged to her mother and was in the envelope with the documents delivered to her at her mother's gravesite. She was the only mourner until the man had arrived. Another mysterious man, another mysterious envelope. She'd received the first messenger letter informing her of her mother's death and the date and time of her graveside service while at practice.

Her father had been furious when she'd made it back to Paris. He'd ranted on and on about security risks and the need to know where she was. Finally, to stop his tirade, she admitted that she'd gone to her mother's funeral and showed him what had been given to her. Well, everything but the ring. She wanted to keep it and wasn't going to risk her father's temper.

Her father never spoke of her mother, so she didn't tell him she'd go to the small town on the coast. He wouldn't have allowed it. Being an adult, she could do what she wanted, yet incurring the displeasure of her father was not an easy thing. She'd walked a fine line all her life. Her father expected her to be the best, to conform to his wishes and not rock the boat. She'd grown up ensuring she not only didn't rock the boat; hell, she barely moved. Her father was strict; he was the absolute power in her life. She'd been whipped with a belt when she misbehaved. She'd been sent away to boarding school and to the States, and still, she loved him, craved his approval, and worked so damn hard for any kindness.

Within the last five years, sitting still so as to not attract her father's attention had become impossible. She'd lived in her own apartment she paid for, had a career she loved, and had made friends. The breathing room and separation from the constant oversight had allowed her to grow and be free. Then she met Heath, and her world blossomed into a joy she never believed she'd have the privilege of receiving. She received his love, approval, kindness, and support without question and without sacrifice. He allowed her to blossom into who she'd become. Still, there was that young girl yearning for her father's affection and approval under the warmth of her relationship with Heath. That scared little girl would probably never go away, no matter how much Heath loved her.

Going to the funeral was a last minute decision. So, she stood beside a casket and a hole in the ground and listened to the priest. The confusion of indifference and sadness she felt watching the coffin lower into the ground was what she'd focused on until she saw the polished brown shoes in front of her. Ysabel looked up as a man handed her an envelope before he walked away without explanation.

She never knew her mother. The woman her father had said would bring nothing but heartbreak had died, and she'd felt ... almost nothing. Ysabel shook her head. She should have mourned the loss of her mom. The loss of a relationship she'd never have, but she didn't. Her father had been her only parent for as long as she could remember. She'd had a privileged life, as he reminded her regularly. Her father was extremely wealthy and had quadrupled his fortune when cryptocurrency was in its infancy. He sent her to the best schools and provided her with the best violin teachers money could buy, yet his time was something she'd never received. So, her love of music filled her life, and she pursued classical violin above all things until Heath came into her life.

"You have roses again."

At her friend Aimee's words, Ysabel looked up from where she was carefully encasing her Stradivarius.

"The same man?"

Ysabel smiled and reached for the card Aimee plucked from the bouquet and handed to her. "Of course, who else sends you flowers?"

Ysabel shook her head and read the note. "He's asking to meet for drinks."

Aimee's eyes grew wide. "Oh, that's new. Where?"

Ysabel handed her the card and finished securing her violin. "I can't."

"Why not? This is in the 16th Arrondissement. It's safe." Aimee handed her back the note. "I can go with you, and if he's weird, we'll leave together. He's sent you roses after every show for the last four months. That should be worth a drink with him, at least." Aimee buried her nose in the roses and drew a breath. "Lovely."

"No. My father would have an aneurysm. You know how he is."

"If we listened to our fathers, none of us would have sex. Besides, he's not paying your bills. Don't let him stop you from having a life, Ysabel. Sex isn't a bad thing. You should try it sometime." Aimee laughed when Ysabel jerked her head in her friend's direction. Aimee laughed loudly and spread her arms open wide. "What? Am I wrong?"

Ysabel lowered her eyes and felt her cheeks heat. "No, not wrong, just loud." Continuing in a whisper as she glanced around the room where the musicians prepared before and after shows, she said, "And I've had sex before."

Aimee leaned into her and glanced toward the few remaining musicians. "I bet they've had sex, too."

Ysabel gave a half-hearted, nervous laugh and picked up her case. "Probably."

"So, are we going?" Aimee grabbed her case. When Ysabel hesitated, Aimee jumped on her toes and squealed. "I'll pay for the car ride."

Ysabel held up her hand. "If he's weird, we're gone, and you can never tell my father." Her father's disdain for everyone was legendary. He wasn't exactly a warm person, and if she made him mad, life could become difficult.

"I promise, and I never see your father. Neither do you, so how will he know?" Aimee made a motion of crossing her heart. "Let's go."

Thirty minutes later, Ysabel knew why her secret admirer had never signed his last name. The man turned out to be a very recognizable and married politician. Of course, Aimee made her excuses and left once she recognized the attractive man as a wealthy, prominent government figure. That was Aimee's definition of not weird, it seemed. Ysabel wasn't amused by her friend's stage wink as she left.

Ysabel attempted to leave with Aimee, but the Assembleé Nationale leader placed his hand over her arm and prevented her from moving. The pleasant smile turned into almost a sneer. "You will have a drink with me. You owe me this much. A frog such as yourself should be honored to be seen with a man like me. Your talent is impressive, and I have a proposition for you."

The truth of his words cut her like a razor blade. She wasn't beautiful like Aimee, but she wasn't the pursuer either. This man had the audacity to insult her after spending four months sending her flowers? Ysabel jerked her arm away. She glanced around, looking for any way to leave the table without making a scene. She hissed, "I owe you nothing."

"I'd say you owe me more than a drink. You accept my gifts." The man poured her a glass of champagne, which she wouldn't touch. A shiver of disgust traveled over her skin.

"There you are. It's good to see you again. Thank you for meeting me here tonight."

Ysabel jumped at the voice beside her. She glanced up at the attractive man. He was unfamiliar but had a kind look in his eyes. Still, she didn't know him. "Ah ..."

"Excuse me, the lady is with me." The politician sneered at the gentleman.

"Really? We have had a date scheduled for several

weeks." The man's confusion appeared sincere. "Right?" he asked her. His American accent coming through clearly in his French. The "r" not being pronounced correctly by Americans was an easy tell.

She scrambled to understand the American was giving her a way out of this situation. When it finally crystallized in her mind, she smiled at him. "Yes. That's right. The gentleman here is the one I told you about who's been sending me flowers after my shows. He suggested I meet him for a drink, and since I knew you'd be here, I thought it wouldn't hurt, but he's been rather insistent." Ysabel lowered her gaze and shot a disgusted look across to the politician.

"Really?" Her savior cocked his head. "The ring on your finger would suggest you're married. My date isn't the type of woman you're after. She has better taste. You should find another who may be grateful for your time and attention. Of course, I'm assuming your wife knows about your pursuits?" The man's words were pointed and a bit too loud, rather like an American. The quiet conversations in the room dimmed even further. The politician glanced around nervously and leaned back. The hatred in his eyes was directed at the man beside her.

"Leave. Now," he hissed.

Ysabel took the opportunity to stand. "What a

marvelous idea. Please don't send me any more flowers. I do not want them." She paused and lowered her voice even further. *"And if you wanted to influence my father, you chose the wrong way. I'll make sure he knows what happened here tonight. Don't expect a contribution to your party."* Ysabel stood up after retrieving her violin case from under the table and walked away with her new friend.

He motioned to a table, and she slid into the booth, placing her violin beside her. She was shaking from the encounter. *"Thank you so much,"* Ysabel spoke in English to him.

He answered in kind. *"Not a problem. It looked like you needed rescuing."*

"How did you know?" Ysabel wasn't ready to jump from the political hot pan into the unknown fire.

"The gentleman who you were sitting with was ..." The American shrugged.

"A jerk," Ysabel said quietly, but the man heard her and smiled.

The waiter came up to them, and her rescuer cocked his head. *"Would you care to have a drink or perhaps dinner?"*

"Let's start with a drink." Ysabel smiled back at the handsome American. He waited for her to give her

order, then ordered the typical American drink. Whiskey.

"What's your name?"

"Heath Morris, and in full disclosure, I want you to know I recognized you when you walked in. I went to the Philharmonie de Paris several months ago and was lucky enough to watch you play as first chair during your performance of Paganini's Twenty-Fourth Caprice. Of course, your name may have been mentioned in the program, but unfortunately, I didn't and still don't remember it."

"I'm Ysabel Archambeau."

He smiled widely. "A beautiful name. A pleasure to make your acquaintance, ma'am."

Ysabel smiled at the typical American greeting. She enjoyed her time in America while she studied music. It was the most interesting time of her life.

When their drinks arrived, they each took a sip. "So, Mr. Morris—"

"Heath, please."

"Heath," she conceded. "What do you do when you're not rescuing damsels in distress and attending classical concerts?"

"I work as a freelance consultant for an American company. A troubleshooter of sorts." The man shrugged.

"It's boring but profitable. May I ask who your father is? You bandied him about like a saber just now."

"Pierre Archambeau." She studied his face, looking for a reaction.

The man took a drink of his whiskey and frowned. "And he's ... important?"

Ysabel laughed at his confusion. "He's wealthy, yes."

"Ah, well, money is a motivator to some, but in reality, when you have enough to do what gives you pleasure, do you need more?"

"I would think not. Do you have enough?" She wasn't being nosey; she was ensuring he wasn't looking for an introduction to her father.

He chuckled. "I do. Would you like to see my bank accounts?"

Her eyes popped open, and she hurried to say, "I didn't mean to offend."

"No, no offense taken. After witnessing what was going on at that table, I assure you I understand why you'd ask. I have no desire to meet your father." He chuckled. "And while I enjoy classical music, I listen to more modern music as a matter of preference. I apologize if either of those statements offends you."

She smiled at him. "No offense taken. Are you in Paris for business?"

"No, I live in Paris most of the year and travel back

to the States and other countries as my business dictates. I own an apartment not far from here, which is why I was fortunate enough to be in the right place at the right time for you tonight."

"Which I appreciate more than you realize. I've never done anything remotely this spontaneous before, but ..."

"He sent flowers and asked nicely?"

She shook her head and sighed. "He sent flowers after every performance for the last four months and never signed his last name. Tonight, he asked to meet for a drink. I thought I was being wise by bringing Aimee with me, but she wasn't much help."

"Well, Mr. Flower's loss is my gain." He lifted his drink in a silent toast.

Ysabel took a sip of hers as well. "His name isn't Flowers."

"Does it concern you I don't care what his name is?" Heath asked as the waiter stopped by again. "Would you like to eat dinner with me? I'm hungry and would love the company."

Ysabel smiled at the man across from her. "I'd be delighted."

. . .

Heath. That first meeting was so random, and they'd visited, ate, and drank until the establishment closed. He called a taxi for her, paid the driver far too much money for the short trip to her home, and watched until the taxi turned the corner. It was the beginning of a whirlwind romance. She'd loved him with a desperation that had initially scared her.

Passion. Ah, the romanticized love she'd read about but had never experienced. It was real, and her passion was reserved for Heath. She knew the universe had delivered him into her orbit for a reason. They were perfect for each other. Others had wanted attention and time she couldn't give them. Not Heath. Somehow, he understood her professional drive and need for perfection in her music. He understood the time her efforts took from her life and supported her. Heath was a breath of fresh air. He allowed her to be herself and loved her even with her imperfections. It was a freedom she'd never had before. Her father wouldn't tolerate anything but perfection, and his standard was impossible to reach. Each triumph she reached in her career and life, he'd belittle and demand more.

The lamp flickered and then died. Ysabel

wrapped herself in the sleeping bag and prayed she wouldn't be forgotten and left to die. There was so much life left to live. *Please, Heath, please forgive me. I love you.*

* * *

The phone rang five minutes after Harbinger hung up with Fury and Anubis. He was expecting the call. Smoke didn't wait for him to say a word before blurting out, "What's going on? Ysabel is missing?"

"Hey. You got the brief quickly." Harbinger dropped and sat down on the chair in his comm room. It wasn't a conversation he wanted broadcast over public frequencies. "Are we secure?"

"Of course." Smoke sounded offended. "What's going on?"

"Her fucking father convinced her to break off the engagement. Something is up with him, Smoke. My gut is telling me what I just saw was a fucking act. I can't trust him. I won't."

"Dude, we've cleared Ysabel as you asked before you proposed. The background on him was suspended when she broke off the engagement. I started it again when Fury called me. We're doing a deep dive into all things Archambeau. CCS and Flack have it as a priority."

"Thank you. Archambeau is a snake. I've always suspected it."

"Yeah, well, somehow, he's now in bed with one of the deadliest men on our scope. Abrasha Molchalin is a bastard of the highest caliber. We've had dealings with him before."

"I gathered by Fury's comments." Harbinger closed his eyes. "She's a pawn, again. Just like she was the first night I met her. I did some digging on that politician. He wanted to use her for her father's connections. He may have been dissuaded." Harbinger had paid the man a visit and ensured Ysabel would never be contacted again.

"You didn't tell me that part. I don't blame you, though. I probably would've done the same thing. But knowing Charley, she would've punched out the guy and then threatened to castrate him if he approached her again."

"Your wife is scary." Harbinger chuckled. The woman was a firecracker and high up in Guardian. How high up, he didn't know and had the sense not to ask.

"She is." Smoke was quiet for a moment before saying, "I knew you'd been watching Ysabel for some time before you approached her that night, right?"

"Yeah. I went to a couple of concerts in disguise." *Try seven.* Harbinger had been so entranced by Ysabel that just watching her play was a treat. He'd wanted to make sure she wasn't married or dating anyone before approaching her. Knowing others in his group had managed to have long-term relationships had given him the thought that maybe, just maybe, if they hit it off, he could make it work. But he was being cautious. What he did for a living wasn't without jeopardy. Everyone he allowed into his life needed to be thoroughly checked out, and he didn't want to ask Guardian to run a background on her if the relationship had no chance of happening. He wasn't sure how to meet her, so he fell back on what he knew and what he was trained to do. He watched who she interacted with, where she went, found out where she lived, and noticed the flowers that were sent to her after every performance. It was the reason he'd delayed meeting her. He followed her to the restaurant that night because she didn't go straight home. That was an anomaly.

"What's your immediate plan?" Smoke asked.

"Fury and Anubis are working it from the

corporate angle. For me, I'm going hunting." He would find the bastard who had her, and he would take him out.

"No, dude. Hunting Molchalin isn't what you need to do right now. Let the big guys plan the mission. I know you want to tear something apart and make it bleed, but if you go after Molchalin, and they think for a minute it's related to the visit her father just paid you. She's dead. You know it, and so do I."

Harbinger leaned forward and ran his hand through his hair. "I feel so fucking helpless, and yeah, I didn't think I'd ever say this, but I *want* to kill the people responsible for this. I'm *going* to kill them. Copy?"

"Yeah, I get it. I do. I've been where you're at. I've killed my way back to Charley. No one is going to take that from you," Smoke reassured him. "But you have to give the Guardian machine time to move. You know as well as I do if a mission isn't constructed with the right assets in the right places, shit will go to hell real quick. Don't move on this. Not yet."

"I can't just sit here." He'd go insane.

"Then call the housekeeper, get your killer cat

back, and in the meantime, I'll send you what information we have on Archambeau. It isn't much. You probably know more than I do. Use your connections in Paris and start them working on what the fucker is doing now. Gather information and work this like a target with no folio from your end. Don't go insane. Help is on the way. That's a promise from me to you. You have my word."

"I'm holding you to that, Smoke."

"You know you can, my friend. Whatever it takes."

"As long as it takes. Just don't take long."

Smoke grunted. "As fast as humanly possible. I'm clear."

Harbinger disconnected and stared at his phone. "One step at a time." Leaning forward, he dialed a number to a very unsavory individual who owed him many favors. They'd never met, but Harbinger was calling in the favors today. The man was connected to every illegal and illicit enterprise in the city. If anyone wanted to know what was happening in the underbelly of Paris, Mathieu would be able to find out.

"My friend, it's been a long time," Mathieu said in English.

"I'm calling in all my favors." Harbinger didn't beat around the bush.

"What is it you need?"

"Pierre Archambeau. I want to know what he's doing and who he's doing it with."

"I assume you mean nonlegitimate business."

"I wouldn't come to you if I didn't."

"When?"

"As soon as humanly possible." He wanted the information now.

"I'll have it to you this time tomorrow."

"I'll call you."

"Good. And this will clear all debt?"

"Yes. All debt," Harbinger assured him before disconnecting.

CHAPTER 4

*H*arbinger stared at his phone and willed it to ring. Guardian was a massive company with a global reach. Smoke was right. Striking out on his own would be stupid, and it would risk Ysabel's safety. So, he waited as his Guardian handlers worked in the background. He glanced at his watch. Nine hours. It was nine hours since he'd called in. They should have something—

A single knock on his door had him up and his weapon off safety. He picked up his phone and hit the app to see who was at his front door. Well, fuck a duck and add a turkey.

He made his way to the door and opened it,

gun still in his hand. "What in the hell are you doing here?"

Valkyrie walked past him. "That's *not* nice. Do you have anything to eat? The selection in Economy sucked."

Smith Young, Val's husband, waited until he was invited in. Harbinger shut the door behind them. "Yeah, the housekeeper brought some groceries earlier. What are you doing here?"

"We're your backup," Smith said as he entered the kitchen.

"Oh, a cat!" Val dropped down and cooed over Spike, who soaked up the attention. Harbinger's housekeeper had brought him back when she delivered the groceries and set up a schedule to clean now that he was back in Paris. "Such a beautiful baby. Is it yours?"

"Yes. His name is Spike, and he'll tolerate that for about thirty seconds."

Val snorted and picked up the cat. "Men." She kissed Spike's head and sat down with him in her lap at the kitchen table. Spike started his motorboat purr and closed his eyes as Val stroked his golden fur. Val turned her attention to him. "Food? I'm starving. I hate traveling Economy."

"Wait, you said *Economy*?" Harbinger blinked at his friends.

"The only two seats available to get us here," Smith said. "I think my knees are permanently bruised."

"No doubt," Harbinger agreed. Smith was a huge man. Harbinger wasn't sure how he'd folded up to fit into an Economy seat.

"So, we got the bare bones brief from Fury as we were running out the door to get here. Anything new?"

"No. I have Pierre's phone, but I've secluded it in a Faraday cage in case it was a plant."

Val stroked Spike and watched her husband forage through the fridge. She nodded. "You don't trust her father?"

"No. Not as far as I can throw him."

"Why?" Smith asked as he pulled food out of the refrigerator.

Harbinger grabbed a bottle of wine as he answered. "Gut feeling. He's alleged to have escaped the grasp of le milieu and is a legit businessman, yet when he needed protection for Ysabel, he contacted the boss. Not an old friend, the main man."

"He's connected. So is Abrasha," Smith said.

Harbinger's head snapped in the big guy's direction. "What?"

Val continued to stroke the cat as she answered. "We've made Abrasha Molchalin our own little project, which is why Guardian sent us. Anya thinks Smith looks like Abrasha."

Harbinger blinked as his mind flashed back to that train ride in Russia. "Your father told your mother you looked just like him? You think the 'him' in the situation was Molchalin?"

Smith nodded. "We pulled in some favors from the CIA and have several old and grainy photographs of him."

Harbinger waited a heartbeat, but no one said anything. "So, do you look like him?"

"He does. Almost identical," Val said as Harbinger handed her a glass of wine. "Smith is in better shape, is more muscular, and taller than Abrasha, but yeah, they share enough characteristics they could be related."

Smith pulled down four plates and started placing fruit and cheese on each. "Who's the fourth plate for?"

"Con," Valkyrie said. "He's coming to oversee all things techie for you."

"Do I know him? Was he on your flight?"

"He's the one who made the ancient one's phone play that kid's tune," Smith said from where he was slicing a baguette.

Valkyrie laughed. "No, none of us has met him. Wait, I think Ice and Mal may have. Anyway, he's flying in from wherever he does his techie stuff. Fury said he'd be here at roughly the same time."

Harbinger handed Smith a glass of wine but didn't take any for himself. He was jonesing for a fight, and alcohol would only increase that desire. "I have the phone with the texts, and if there were calls between Abrasha and Pierre, it should be on there, too. It was supposed to be his personal phone."

Smith frowned. "And he gave it up?"

Harbinger stared at the man and smirked. "Without hesitation."

Val stopped petting Spike. "Odd, isn't it? I mean, if Abrasha is sending proof of life photos to that number…"

"It's conceivably the only way Abrasha can contact him. Yeah, that's why it's in a Faraday cage in my comm room." Harbinger thought it was sketchy as hell.

Smith pulled out a chair and sat down with his lunch after placing Val's and his on the table.

"Flack and I will continue working on a file on Abrasha and now Archambeau. There's little to nothing readily available on Molchalin, so we're using alternative methods to gather as much information as possible. Archambeau will be by the numbers until we discover anything unsavory."

"Alternative methods?" Harbinger picked at the food in front of him. He wasn't hungry. His gut was twisted in ten different knots, and all felt like they'd been drenched in acid. He had to find Ysabel.

"That's code for the dark side," Val said while eating a piece of cheese. She broke off a tiny piece for Spike and fed it to him.

"The dark web—or dark net, whichever you prefer. Con will be using your comm room while I work with Flack in ours. Fury assumed your comm room was secure," Smith clarified.

"Our comm room most definitely is, and our place isn't too far from here. Who knew we were neighbors?" Val took a sip of wine. "God, I needed this. Economy." She shivered and took another sip of her wine.

"Yeah, my comm room is secure."

"Good, then Con will stay with you and work from this location, and Smith will connect with

Flack. With both of them working, we'll figure out what's up with Abrasha and use everything we have to find your woman." Val set her glass down. "Which reminds me. Don't think you're going to get out of the trouble you're in with us. You could have said something, jerk. Engaged, really?"

"Right, because you were so upfront with your relationship. You kidnapped him and flew him to Europe. Did you tell anyone before you did that?" Harbinger pointed at Smith as he talked.

Smith looked at his wife. "He has a point."

"No, he doesn't. It wasn't *really* kidnapping. You went willingly. Besides, at that point, we didn't know we were in love." She pointed at Harbinger. "He *did*. He asked her to marry him! Like that was twenty steps ahead of us at that time."

Smith swiveled his head back and looked at Harbinger. "She has a point."

He frowned at his friend. "Dude, just eat. I don't need you to keep score."

Val laughed. "Afraid I'm going to win?"

"I love a good competition," said a man he'd never seen before from his kitchen doorway.

Harbinger, Val, and Smith were up with three automatics trained on the guy before he could blink. The cat scurried out of the kitchen past the stranger. The man laughed and pointed at the cat. "He took out of ..." The guy turned around, saw the guns, and lifted his hands slowly. "Whoa. My name is Con. You invited me here. The front door was unlocked, and I'm hungry." He pointed toward the front door before swiveling his index fingers to point at the extra plate on the counter.

"Jesus, man, ever think to knock?" Harbinger said, his weapon still trained on the guy.

"The door was *unlocked*. Why knock?"

Harbinger leveled his weapon at the man. "Prove you're Con."

The man rolled his eyes. "Y'all know the song I put on the Ancient One's phone?"

All heads went north and south. Con started singing the song about a baby shark.

Smith was the first to drop his weapon but lifted it again. "Stop singing that, or I'll shoot you just because."

Con's mouth snapped shut. Valkyrie returned her weapon to her boot from where she'd pulled it and waved a hand. "Your food is over on the counter."

"Cool, a picnic. I'll eat and work if you take me to the phone and your comm room. I know you want answers ASAP."

Harbinger was down with that. His cell phone rang in his pocket. "Go."

"Authenticate Messenger." Fury's voice came over the phone.

"Heralder," he replied. "Con, Val, and Smith are here."

"Good. Put me on speaker."

He did what he was told, and Fury continued. "We were able to confirm Pierre Archambeau's story that Ysabel was born in the States. The background check Harbinger had run on her before he proposed validated her American birth but nothing else. Since then, we've discovered her original birth certificate was produced at the county hospital and filed at the courthouse. They have it on microfiche, which has since been digitized. No father was listed on the birth certificate, but Léonie is listed as the mother. The adoption was legal … ish."

"What do you mean *ish?*" Smith asked before he could.

"The lawyer who did the private adoption died before he could file the documents with the court. So, while the paperwork was done, it was never registered with the court."

"It doesn't matter, does it? She's an adult."

"But she isn't Pierre's daughter. She's Abrasha's, allegedly, which means he has two heirs. Both daughters, both by the same woman."

"What?" Val asked.

"You heard that right. Ysabel has a sister, five years younger, and Abrasha hasn't made a move from his location in Switzerland, but his daughter has."

"Switzerland? They haven't kicked him out yet?" Con asked.

"No," Fury answered bluntly. "The daughter is in Paris and has been since her mother's death."

A sudden thought struck Harbinger. "Question."

"What?" Fury bit out the response.

"Why didn't the second daughter or the old man himself attend the mother's funeral? Are we sure she's dead? What information would she give Ysabel that Abrasha and his other daughter would want or go after? Why crypto, and why the hell would Pierre be their target?"

"All good questions. Jewell wants your tech guy to contact her as soon as he gets set up."

"Got it. The name's Con, by the way. In case you forgot," Con snarked.

There was a muffled response, and Con snickered from his position in the middle of the kitchen.

Harbinger wasn't going to get into their pissing contest. Instead, he asked, "How did you locate the sister? I could've done that for you."

"We have an asset from the baby class in Paris. Jinx will remain in the area should we need his assistance. To this point, we have a fuckton of questions and no information. Tear that phone apart and get us some answers. Conference call in six hours, and the big guy will be on board for this one. Val and Smith have new comm earpieces for both of you. Be ready."

Con picked up his plate and took Valkyrie's glass of wine. "Hey, get your own." She grabbed it back. "Besides, you're working." She tossed the guy a small black case. "Your earpiece."

"Damn." Con sighed after he caught the case. "Okay, take me to your comm room."

Harbinger was more than happy to set the guy up, and after he caught his earpiece, he motioned for Con to follow him. Con stopped and picked up a small suitcase before following Harbinger into the communications area Harbinger had built.

"This will do nicely."

"The bed and bathroom connected are yours to use."

"Thanks. I'll let you know as soon as I have something." Con went in and dropped the suitcase he was carrying. "Phone?"

"There." Harbinger pointed to the small box on the counter.

"Cool." The guy popped a piece of cheese into his mouth and opened his bag, pulling out the ugliest laptop ever. The thing looked a thousand years old, was boxy, and scratched to hell.

"What's that shit? Guardian can't afford a new one for you?"

"Nah, man, this baby is state of the art. She'll run circles around anything on the market."

"Then why does it look like shit?"

"Man, don't piss off my pretty princess here. She's sensitive, and I made her look this way. If you saw this, would you steal it?"

Harbinger snorted, "No."

"Exactly. Now, give me ten minutes, and I'll have this phone done."

He backed out of the room as Con set up his system. *Finally*, they were going to get some answers.

CHAPTER 5

Ysabel heard the footsteps and sat up on the cot. A flashlight blinded her, and she blinked, turned her head, and held up her hand to protect herself from the light. After so long in the absolute darkness of her little prison, the small flashlight was too bright. "Stay there. Don't move." The words were hissed in French as the door opened.

Batteries were tossed in her direction, along with a cardboard box that was upended and scattered across the dirt floor. The bucket was picked up, and a new one dropped on the floor. The man moved to the door again.

"Wait, tell me what's happening, please. Tell me why I'm here!" She asked the question in French and English, but there was no response. There was never a response.

The door shut, and she was once again entombed in darkness. Carefully, she slid off the bed and in the direction the batteries were thrown. It took forever to find them and then to replace them in complete darkness. Ysabel broke into tears several times but found the drive to keep trying. When the light came on, she knocked the lamp off her lap. The intense brightness burned her eyes. Ysabel took off her shirt and draped it over the light before opening her eyes a little. Red and white splotches still danced in front of her eyes, but she was able to tolerate the dimmed shadows in her cell. She moved slowly and collected the food and water bottles that scattered from the box tossed at her.

She opened the first wrapped package and ate the stale bread. There was no nutrition in the food she was given. No rhyme or reason as to what she received. Biscuits, crisps, candy, sugary nuts, bread. Yet it was food, so she ate. She guzzled the first bottle of water. It'd been a long time since she'd had any. Or so she thought. Ysabel upended the box and put her food on the top.

A rat scurried from under her cot, over her

foot, across the floor, and up the wall. She screamed and jumped onto a stone ledge. The disgusting vermin wedged itself through a crack in the wall. Ysabel searched the floor and grabbed stones before she ran across the small space and crammed the rocks into the fissure the rat had disappeared into. She tore off a big piece of the box and shoved it behind the stones. If the thing came back, she'd know. She grabbed several palm-sized stones and piled them near where she slept.

She flipped the cot over and lifted the sleeping bag, still holding a rock in her hand. Nothing. Thank you, God. Righting her cot, she put the bag back on top of it and sat down. Her head ached, and her eyes hurt. After getting into the bag, she reached over to turn off the lamp. She should save the batteries. Leaving her shirt on the lamp would prevent her from frying her retinas again—she hoped.

Ysabel called to mind happier times. Times with Heath. She smiled into the dark as she recalled the beauty and warmth of one of their dates.

Heath laughed as she tried to guess their destination. Surely, it was a visit to a vineyard in the area. The countryside flew by as they drove to what he promised to be an unforgettable time. When he crested a low hill, she saw the hot air balloon for the first time. The mix of blues and green with a curl of lilac was breathtaking as it sat in the middle of a low meadow.

"Is that for us?" She pointed to the balloon like an excited schoolgirl. She'd always wanted to ride in one.

"It is. Dinner, champagne, and a flight over the countryside."

Ysabel launched across the sedan's console and hugged the man beside her. She kissed his cheek. "Thank you!"

The rest of the road trip seemed to take forever as the balloon grew. She vibrated with anticipation. He helped her from the car to the balloon, her heels completely inappropriate for the field where the balloon waited. When she sunk down into the earth, he tossed the keys to the car to a gentleman and picked her up, carrying her to the incredibly large gondola.

"This is much bigger than I imagined." She carefully found her feet as he released her.

"It's a commercial sightseeing balloon, but I rented it out for the day," Heath said as he motioned to the table with a white cloth and two silver place settings. A stand with a bucket of ice and champagne stood waiting for them.

After a quick introduction to the crew and pilots,

they were lifting into the air. Heath stood beside her, his arm around her waist as the burner engaged in short bursts. They were served champagne as they drifted higher.

"Look." She pointed to a small village. The roofs formed a patchwork of different shades of terra-cotta tiles surrounding the village center. The sound of a church bell tolled, and she could hear a dog barking in the distance. As they drifted over the low, rolling hills, rows of lavender stretched as far as she could see. The fragrance was unbelievable.

"Beautiful," she whispered, almost afraid to intrude on the peacefulness.

Heath turned to her. "The beauty of the land can't compete with you."

She blinked at his words. "I'm not beautiful." Which was the truth. Her features were too sharp; her mouth too big; she was too tall, too thin, and far too plain to be beautiful.

"Beauty is in the eyes of the beholder. The lavender fields are just lines of purple, yet you see the glory of the whole. What one person sees as unremarkable, another sees as majestic and awe-inspiring. You fill me with awe. You are vibrant, animated, resplendently kind, and dazzlingly talented, and you make me want you in a way no one else has. You take my breath away."

Heath shimmered behind the tears that filled her eyes. "Please. Don't tease me."

He stepped closer and pushed her hair behind her ear. His hand cupped her cheek. "I only speak the truth. I will never lie to you. You are incredibly beautiful to me, and I desire you in ways I won't speak of here, but I want you to know how I feel." *He placed her hand on his chest over his heart.*

She stared at him. He returned her gaze, and she saw the sincerity in his eyes. "You make me believe things I shouldn't." *That she was beautiful and that he desired her weren't ideas she readily accepted. She'd been pursued for her talent by men who wanted to be seen with the first chair violinist, not her. There had been others who'd wanted her for her father's money. Both types made themselves known sooner rather than later. Heath had been very sincere in showing her he would benefit from neither association. The meetings between Heath and her father were tense and stilted. Her father automatically disliked Heath and accused him of seeking wealth. Heath laughed in her father's face.* "I have more money than I'll ever need. I didn't even know who you were before I met Ysabel, and I'm a foreigner. I want nothing to do with your political connections or business. You could drop off the face of *the globe, and I wouldn't care. I don't need or want a thing from you."*

"Except my daughter," Pierre hissed at him.

"I already have her." Heath put his arm around Ysabel. "And that's something you can't stop."

She'd endured an hour long tirade after that meeting. Ysabel listened, but for the first time, her father's shouting didn't tear her down. Heath's words of love and encouragement battled every insult and demand slung her direction.

And there she was, floating over the beauty of France, with a man she adored. Could that be her world? Could that be her life? Did she dare to hope? He lowered for a kiss.

"Believe those things, Ysabel. Believe in me. Just believe."

Ysabel wiped a tear as it fell. In the darkness, she could mourn for the love she'd thrown away. If only he knew the reason why she'd turned him away. The shock, then the pain she'd witnessed that night, had put a lance through her heart, but he would *live*. He would be protected from her mother's delusions. Why had she sent the envelope with no documents? Were the documents stolen before the messenger delivered them to her? She had no answers and so many questions.

Her father should be looking for her if he were still alive. She'd heard the men in Corsica talking about Abrasha Molchalin as if he were a demi-god. They were amazed at the things the man was behind and rumored to control. The fact Molchalin was her biological father was such a foreign concept, yet it explained the physical differences between her dad and herself. As she grew, she eclipsed his five feet seven inches. Her bone structure was sharper, and she was naturally thin, whereas her father had to diet and exercise to maintain his health. Things she didn't question until she saw the letter from her mother. Her mother gave birth to her in America, so she had dual citizenship and attended Juilliard, focusing on her music.

Yet nothing she knew was true. Her world had been tipped on its axis, and looking back, the only sliver of her reality that was as it seemed was Heath. He was a breath of honesty and integrity. There were no shades of truth, no lies, or subterfuge with him. To keep him from harm from her father's enemies and her mother's missing information, she'd rejected him. Her father was right on that one point, and it resonated through her soul. Heath was a businessman, innocent, and yet by his association with her, he was in grave danger. He'd be hurt just because he loved her. She couldn't allow that to happen. Yes, she'd thrown his love away to protect him. She'd do it again.

CHAPTER 6

Harbinger walked into his comm room and stopped short. Con's arms were crossed, and his head was down on the desk. A soft snore carried to where Harbinger stood. He glanced at the phone, which was disassembled beside the man. Con's computer ran with some script flashing across the screen. Harbinger walked up behind him and opened the Faraday box, closing the lid as soon as he saw a small computer chip inside.

So, the phone was bugged. The rage he felt at being played by Pierre was nothing compared to the hatred he'd wield if he found out the man was using his daughter as a pawn. There was no way that photo of Ysabel was anything but original. He could see the terror in her eyes; those bruises weren't makeup. They couldn't be.

Con's head popped up. "What?"

Harbinger lifted an eyebrow as the man pulled his computer to him without even looking at Harbinger.

"No, I grabbed a couple of minutes of sleep. It's been about seventy-two hours since I last powered down." Con finally saw him out of the corner of his eye and damn near jumped out of his skin. "Fuck, dude, knock next time?"

Harbinger cocked his head. "My house, I don't have to knock, and the door was unlocked."

"No, it's H. He's here. Has it been six hours?" Con looked at his watch and then yawned. "Okay." He glanced over at Harbinger. "Are Val and Smith here?"

"No, they went to their place and will patch in from there." Harbinger sat down in front of the screen where the video call would take place.

"Hear that?" Con asked whoever was on the other end of his earpiece. "Yeah, give me a sec."

Con ran his hand through his sleep-strewn hair and yawned. Then he dropped his hands and started typing faster than Harbinger had seen anyone type before. The screen activated, and

Jewell King appeared on the screen. She waved, and her voice came over the speaker. "Patching everyone in. Standby."

Harbinger nudged Con's chair with his boot. "Anything good on that?"

"Oh hell, yeah," Con whispered.

"Archangel online," Jewell said, and the screens started to populate as each of the other sections checked in.

"Sunset Operative Thirteen and Bravo online," Val chimed in.

Harbinger announced his and Con's presence after Fury, Anubis, and Alpha announced they were present.

Archangel leaned forward. "I have a bare-bones brief in front of me. Harbinger, how did Pierre Archambeau know to come to you for help?"

"He played hide and go seek with Archambeau's private dicks." Fury provided the answer. "So, of course, the guy thought he was James freaking double oh seven or something."

"All right. Taking that at face value, what have we learned or accomplished in the last six hours?"

Harbinger started the conversation, "There was a man watching my building. He didn't move when Val, Smith, or Con entered. They left, and he stayed, so I'm assuming he was told to sit on me. I went out and came back in. He didn't follow. After that, I put on a disguise and made my way out. The guy grunted and kept looking toward the street."

"Where is he now?" Alpha asked.

Con jolted and moved to the computer system. Harbinger put his hand on Con's shoulder and shook his head. "Still downstairs as of three minutes ago in a black sedan that pulled up right after I bumped into him the second time." Con instantaneously relaxed.

"We've taken a lot of information off the phone. The photos were sanitized and had no geo markers attached to them, but based on the background, you can tell Ysabel is being held in a very dark area. The flash of the camera barely punctuated past her person. What we can see is stone and a lot of it."

"Specifically, limestone," Con added.

"Correct, which leads to the massive assumption she's being held in the catacombs," Jewell said as she typed. "We reached out to our sources, one of whom is a Cataphile."

"A what?" Val asked.

"Cataphile. They're a society of about three hundred people who enter the non-public areas of the catacombs and explore. Completely illegal, mind you. There have been massive bars and cinemas placed in the catacombs. Of course, when they're found out, they're shut down. There are over two hundred miles of passages dug through the limestone. A very small portion is maintained and open to the public."

"How do we find her?" Harbinger leaned forward, his elbows on his knees.

"Unfortunately, that would be like looking for a needle in a haystack." Fury shook his head. "What other information did you get from the phone?"

Jewell answered, "The first picture was sent from a different telephone number than the second. Again, a burner phone. Service was paid for in cash, and the phone was reported as one of the thousands of phones stolen when the pirates off the Strait of Malacca in Indonesia ransacked that freighter."

"And why is that important, you ask?" Con interjected. "Well, thank you for that question," he answered himself. "The pirates who stopped and raided that freighter have ties to the Russian Mafia." Con smiled at Harbinger like he'd just blown the case open.

"So?" Harbinger asked.

"So? Dude, Abrasha Molchalin is Russian."

"That's like saying because I'm American, I'm involved with the mob," Fury snapped.

Jewell shook her head. "No, it isn't. You haven't been connected to the mob. AM has been."

"AM?" Alpha asked.

"It's too flipping hard saying his name all the time. Besides, that's what Smith calls him," Jewell said. "Anyway, according to the information provided by the CIA, the ring of pirates in that area of Indonesia was alleged to be funded by the Russian Mafia. That's where they got their guns, boats, and training."

"How does that tie Abrasha to the phone?" Alpha asked.

"We assumed the money used to fund the pirates was moved through the shell company shuffle. We didn't look at the obvious—a bank. One bank in particular is in Switzerland. Plume Pharma's bank."

Fury blurted, "You're shitting me."

"I am not," Jewell said, continuing, "As we're learning, Plume Pharma has no income from their business in Switzerland. They do, however, receive huge amounts of money from various Plume holdings. Then, they send money internationally to small satellite facilities. One of which is on a tiny island on the Strait of Malacca. This year, it has received over one million dollars and has two employees. A receptionist and a security guard."

Archangel leaned forward and growled, "When did you find this information? This indicates a conduit."

"About three hours ago. When we were researching the phone heist. We wouldn't have seen the connection if we hadn't just had a mission in France that included Plume." Jewell clapped her hands together. "But we saw the transfer, and he could be paying the pirates."

"That doesn't help Ysabel." Harbinger had enough of the extra shit going on. It wasn't the focus of the conference call.

"But it could!" Jewell said. "He's using his companies to fund his efforts. What's to say he's not funding whatever's going on in Paris with Plume or one of the other of his companies?"

"How long would it take you to find a connection?" Fury asked.

"If we have permission to go dark, a week, maybe two."

"She might not have that long." Harbinger

stood up and started pacing. "What else do we have?"

"Her father called three unregistered numbers right before he came to see you," Con said. "We tried to call those numbers. All three failed to answer our random and changing number from the Paris exchange. There was a tracker in his phone; however, where it was placed was strange. It was almost as if it had been manufactured that way." Con picked up a large piece of the phone with wires attached to it running to his computer. "This still works. If he gets a call, we can answer it. If he gets a text, we can see it and trace it back if the person who sends it doesn't turn off their phone. At a minimum, we hope we can get a cell phone tower location."

"We confirmed a death certificate for Léonie was issued in Switzerland. There's a burial site and headstone also."

Harbinger's attention snapped to the screen. "So, the funeral Ysabel attended was a setup?"

"The company that dug the hole in France was paid in cash, and the casket was empty, but they didn't care. The priest was contacted via email and offered a big gratuity to perform the service when it happened. It had been set up for over six months. The priest was told the date and made the trek to the gravesite. Nothing can be traced. We don't have any information on the alleged messenger," Jewell noted.

"What about the heist Pierre says Abrasha wants him to orchestrate?" Harbinger asked.

Jewell sighed, "Unfortunately, we need more information."

"He said there was a list of businesses and people who would be targeted and that the devices the crypto was held on would be stolen and provided to him," Harbinger repeated the information Pierre had told him.

Con turned to him. "At a minimum, we need the list."

"Righto," Jewell added.

"Stealing those devices, or fobs as they're called, will take a highly experienced thief." Archangel rubbed his chin. "I'll contact our resident expert and find out who could do it. The community of people that skilled is small."

"They might not be physical fobs. They could be digital, which is now the norm. My bet is they're digital," Jewell informed the big guy.

"I'd rather have too much information than not enough," Archangel said. "I'll still ask."

"And in the meantime?" Harbinger wanted to pull his hair out by the roots.

"We need proof of life," Fury said. "With a newspaper that shows a date. Hopefully, we can get a cell tower ping at a minimum. Then we enlist our cave dweller—"

"Cataphile," Jewell and Con said at the same time.

"What the fuck ever," Fury growled. "We get that guy to tell us where the entrances in that location are, and we start searching for her."

"We?" Harbinger asked.

"I can help," Smith offered. "Flack would be able to do the research needed without me. CCS can pick up whatever slack is left."

Fury nodded on the screen. "That's one. Jinx is two if you need him, and you would be three. Any more than that, and you'll leave tracks. We don't need the French government involved in this."

"H, get ahold of Pierre and tell him to ask for proof of life and a copy of that list," Archangel commanded. "Con, clone that phone and give it to Harbinger to take to Pierre."

"You got it," Con agreed instantly.

"For some reason, they need Pierre to crack

these encrypted devices. Jewell, what kind of tech does the man need to do that?"

"One hell of a super processor," Con said under his breath.

"What Con said." Jewell nodded. "*We* have the capability; not many do, but then again, we haven't been tracking who has what supercomputer access. And then he'll need to have some damn fine operators. Ones he trusts not to reroute the crypto for themselves."

"Could you override his operators?" Alpha asked.

Both Con and Jewell stopped typing. "What?" they asked in unison.

Alpha shrugged. "Do we trust Pierre?"

"No," everyone answered at once.

"Then we need to be able to ensure the crypto goes where *we* want it to go. Into the account and out of the account when we have Ysabel's location and ensure she's safe. Also, I have two teams in France. One is on alert, but that mission may not materialize. If you need backup, they'll be there."

"Has anyone ever told you you're so much smarter than your brother?" When Con put his hand over his chest and batted his eyes, Harbinger sneered. It wasn't the time to be fucking playing.

"Con…" Archangel warned the operator.

"Sorry. Old habits." Con apologized and completed some type of cross maneuver in front of himself.

"What teams?" Fury asked as he flipped off the screen. Everyone knew who the gesture was for. Con smiled wickedly.

"Delta and Tango."

"Turn Giovanni loose on Pierre." Fury sneered. "She's been on Tango for a couple of years now."

"We aren't interrogating prominent French citizens. *Yet*." Archangel sighed. "Hold that idea, though. Harbinger, I know this is hard. I know it seems like we're sitting on our hands, but we're not. Alpha, send Giovanni's team to Corsica. See if they can find out something from the people who were supposed to be guarding Ysabel down there."

Fury's face split in a smile. "Are we starting a war with the mob?"

"A war? No. A precision strike, yes," Archangel said and leaned forward. "Harbinger, we will find her, and when we do, I promise you whoever is responsible will pay."

Harbinger leveled a stare at the big guy. "As long as I'm at the register when they cash out."

"Smoke and I have talked. I'm of the same mind

as he is. Your request to cash out the individuals involved is granted … if the situation requires it. Archangel clear." The screen went black.

"H, get over to Pierre's," Fury said. "Everyone else has their assignments. We convene again in twelve hours. I want movement on this issue. The Rose is clear."

"Alpha clear."

"Yeah, we're clear, too," Val said.

Jewell was the last on the screen. "Con, get the phone cloned and sleep for a couple of hours. I'll keep everything going. Ethan and I are available to work it if the proof of life or a call happens."

"That's a deal," Con said. "Until then." Con turned to him. "Give me a few minutes."

"I have something to do. I'll be back for it," Harbinger said and headed to the primary bedroom and the secret room behind his walk-in closet. It was time to become someone else.

CHAPTER 7

The reflection in the mirror was unrecognizable. Bald, with brown eyes, a red-hued beard, four inches taller, and wearing a suit, Harbinger called a limo service and ordered a vehicle to pick him up. He checked his makeup closely, looking at the adhesion of the prosthetic nose and the foundation covering the glue. He glanced at his watch and headed back to the communications room, locking his private area and moving his clothes back to hide the entrance even further.

Harbinger made sure to walk in a swagger completely different from his normal stride. Con turned around at the sound of his approach. The man jumped off the stool and grabbed his bag. He whipped out an automatic pistol and held it on Harbinger. "Who the fuck are you?"

"The person letting you stay here, so don't shoot me, asshole."

Con blinked rapidly, and then his jaw almost hit the floor. "Harbinger? How the hell did you do that in ... twenty minutes?"

"Practice. Do you have the cloned phone?"

"Yeah, right here." Con gave the phone to him and then narrowed his eyes. "Man, that shit is spooky. Your eyes don't even look the same."

"Contacts and face tape." Harbinger placed the cloned phone in his inside breast pocket. "Get some sleep."

"That won't be a problem," Con said as he turned back to the workbench. "I've been looking into the catacombs. Specifically, the type of limestone produced from them. I'm ninety-nine-point-nine percent sure the background we saw in her photo is the same type of limestone."

"How?" Harbinger walked up behind the tech guru.

"I sent pictures of the limestone to a geologist who's done work for Guardian. It took him less than five minutes to identify the rock as Lutetian limestone, which is the ancient name given to the limestone of this area by the Romans. He found two distinct gastropods in the pictures that are only found in the Parisian area, so we're in the right geographic area."

"You did that all in twenty minutes?" Harbinger returned the guy's question.

"No, I wish. I sent the pictures before I fell asleep waiting for the conference call." Con rolled his shoulders. "I'm brain dead right now, or I'd start working on …" Con stopped and jumped over to his stool. "Incoming call." He started typing furiously. "Yes, I see it, I'm on it."

Harbinger glanced at the man, then noticed his comm device in his ear.

Con stared at his screen. "Yeah, come on, leave a voice message. I need ten more seconds …" Con stared at the screen and then pumped his fist in the air. "One tower." He pointed to a set of numbers, then sighed before swearing. "No voice message, but we have a ping on this tower. Let me call it up on the map."

Harbinger stared at the map overlay that came up on Con's computer. "That's the 14th

Arrondissement. It's also where the legal entry to the catacombs is located."

"That doesn't help much, then, does it?" Con rubbed his face.

"It gives a place to start. Is there any way to get a list of the unofficial entrances to the catacombs?" Harbinger asked, straightening his jacket.

Con cocked his head. "There should be, right? I mean, if there's a society of people who enter the tunnels on the regular …" Con yawned until his jaw cracked and then started typing.

"Give it to one of the others to look up. Get some sleep, or you'll be no good to anyone," Harbinger said as he moved to look at the screen with the monitors to the building on it. There was a new man sitting in the car outside the door. Harbinger narrowed his eyes at the individual. Why? As far as he knew, there weren't any photographs of him, and he would make damn sure there weren't any.

"What's wrong?"

"Wondering what the person on this building is there for."

"You, probably."

"But there are no photographs of me, and I was right in front of the other man earlier."

Con frowned. "Maybe they're waiting for someone to come *into* the building, not leave it."

Harbinger's eyebrows rose as he snapped a picture of the new man with the camera currently monitoring him. "Have your people run that for facial rec, please. There's another picture with the first man on the desktop."

"I'll find it. Do what you need to do, and then please turn back into you. This thing you got going on now is just … weird."

Harbinger chuffed out a laugh. "Get some sleep."

"Maybe, but not right away. You made my brain wake up. I'm going to pop over to the dark side and see if any of my contacts know about the cataphiles."

Harbinger glanced at the cameras once more and headed downstairs. The limo he'd ordered hadn't arrived yet, so he paced up and down the walk while pulling out a cigarette. He made a show of patting his suit pockets before turning to the man whose entire mission seemed to be watching the door. He tapped on the window and made a motion for the driver to roll down the window. In fluent French, without a trace of an accent, he asked if the man had a lighter. Harbinger had seen him light up earlier, and the cigarette in his hand was his ticket to talk to the man.

The guy stuck his cigarette in his mouth and reached into his pocket, giving Harbinger a glimpse of his automatic settled snuggly under his arm as he took out his lighter. After lighting his cigarette, Harbinger drew a long drag of nicotine and resisted the impulse to cough. He blew out the stream of smoke and let his shoulders drop.

"Nice day," he commented as he handed it back.

The man shrugged and started to roll up the window. Okay, so he wasn't going to be communicative. The guy's eyes kept darting to the street, assessing each of the cars that drove by.

"Waiting on someone?"

The man's eyes snapped to Harbinger, and the window stopped moving up. "Why do you ask?"

Harbinger laughed. "My apologies; I assumed because you were parked here, you were waiting for someone."

"No." The guy finished rolling up the window, crossed his arms over his chest, and stared resolutely toward the street. Harbinger's limo pulled up, and he took a final drag off his cigarette before flicking it into the middle of the road and getting into the back seat of his car. As the vehicle pulled away, Harbinger watched to see if the man would retrieve his cigarette. It was what he'd do if he were tracking someone and didn't know for sure who his target was. DNA was definitive. But the man didn't move. Harbinger turned around and rested against the seat.

His car dropped him off in front of Archambeau's office building. Harbinger went in and was stopped by a security point. "May I ask who you are here to see?"

"Pierre Archambeau." His French once again held an American accent.

"May I ask your appointment time?"

"I don't have an appointment. Tell him a friend of Heath Morris is here to see him."

The security point was on the phone a second later. Harbinger took in the sparse decoration and furnishing of the first-floor entry area. Although the building was modern, it was ... empty. He swept the camera system, noting there were no screens at the security checkpoint. So, security was separated from the holding area where he currently stood. The doors behind the sentry that had greeted him appeared to be wooden, but he'd bet his year's wages they were bulletproof and alarmed.

The guard put down the phone and said, "Please, follow me, sir."

He fell into step behind the suited-up security specialist and notched a mental check in the correct box when he saw the vault-like door open. The protected interior of the building was furnished in dark brown, leather, and gold. He was led to an elevator, and the guard swiped a card held to his belt with a plastic-coated wire. "You'll be met at your floor." The guard stepped out, and the door shut behind him. Harbinger didn't glance at the camera but stared forward. When the car stopped and the doors opened, another security guard was there.

"Sir, I'm going to have to pat you down and ensure you don't have any transmitters on you."

Harbinger stepped out of the elevator and lifted his arms, silently giving the man permission. He waited while the man did his job and then followed him down the hall. There was no receptionist, just a long hall of doors. The security specialist stopped at one door, knocked, and looked up into the camera. The door lock clicked, and the guard stepped aside. "I'll be here when you need to leave."

When he entered the office, Pierre Archambeau

looked up from a desk that sat in the middle of a windowless office. "You have a message for me?" The man didn't look a thing like he did last night at his apartment. His suit was crisp, no wrinkles. His hair was neatly combed, and the haggard look had disappeared. Harbinger's supposition that the entire event had been an act was reinforced.

He walked forward and handed Archambeau the cloned phone. In a voice higher in pitch than his, he said, "You must ask for proof of life, and Mr. Morris wants the list of accounts with names."

"I don't call them. They call me. I don't have the list here." The man took the phone and placed it on his desk.

"If that were true, you wouldn't have left your only means of communication with Mr. Morris, would you? Contact them. Get the list to him. It is not optional."

Pierre's eyes narrowed. "How do you know Mr. Morris?" Pierre stared at him with a hostile glare.

"Proof of life, Mr. Archambeau, and the list. Get it done." Harbinger turned around and headed to the door without answering his question.

Pierre called from behind him. "Do you work for the government?"

Harbinger didn't break stride. Pierre's desire to

know if he worked for the government was becoming an obsession. He opened the door and waited for the security specialist to power walk back to him. "This way, sir." The man held an arm out in the direction they'd come from.

Harbinger left the building, and his waiting car pulled away from the curb with him securely ensconced a few seconds later. Traffic was horrendous, but it always was in Paris. Harbinger rolled down the security window and instructed the driver, "Take the long way back. I'm in no hurry, and your fee will be bigger." After the driver acknowledged the order, Harbinger put the security divider back and swiveled so he could assess if he were being followed. He watched for over twenty minutes before he was satisfied Archambeau was caught flat-footed and hadn't been able to have one of his minions follow him.

His cell phone rang. He retrieved it and swiped the face. "Go."

"I've found a guy who will take you and one other down. I didn't tell him what we were looking for. He said if we have the money, he'll spend the next month showing us everything he knows about the tunnel system." Con yawned again. "Sorry, man."

"You've done well. Leave the contact information. I'll instruct the driver to return immediately."

"Oh, yeah, there's a second thing. The guy in front of the building is a known member of the Corsican mob. So is the dude in the other picture." Con yawned again. "Fuck, sorry, dude. I'm crashing hard."

"I'll be there shortly. Get some sleep." Harbinger hung up without waiting for a response. Con had been working his ass off, and it had paid out. Corsican mob ... Why would the people who were hired to protect Ysabel be watching his apartment building? A piece of the puzzle that didn't yet fit. He dialed Val's number because he didn't have Smith's.

"Go," she said by way of greeting.

"Tell Smith to put on his spelunking gear."

"When?"

"One hour."

"See you then." Val hung up, and Harbinger stared out of the back of the limo. Ysabel ... He wasn't sure what she'd become involved in, but one thing he couldn't shake was the idea her father was deeply involved. The man reeked of complicity. It was an intangible skill Harbinger had honed over his career with Guardian. He could smell it on a person—the acid-like stench of someone guilty of crimes against weaker people. For money, fame, love, or a combination of those three, people would do the most heinous things imaginable—even fathers.

CHAPTER 8

Ysabel jerked awake and listened to the silence of her prison. What had startled her? She reached over for her rock and turned on the lamp, shattering the darkness. With her rock back and ready to throw, she shot her gaze up to the hole where the rat had disappeared. It was still blocked.

There.

She heard someone coming. The voice of her jailer yelled in French, "Stay away from the door!"

Ysabel put her hand holding the large stone behind her back and waited. It wasn't long since he'd last come. She still had food and water.

The door opened, and she blinked at the brightness of the flashlight. "Stand up."

"Why?" she asked.

The man didn't ask again. He walked over and grabbed her arm, jerking her from the cot. "Hold this." He slapped a newspaper at her chest, but it dropped, and he stooped to pick it up. With every ounce of strength she had, Ysabel crashed the rock down on the back of the man's head. He went down to his hands and knees, and the flashlight skittered across the room. Ysabel jumped past the man, grabbed the flashlight, and pushed the door closed behind her. The iron bar that sealed the door shut was heavy and awkward, but she managed to shove it into place. She glanced back through the small window. The man had fallen to the ground and wasn't moving. Had she killed him? She swallowed hard and turned away from the cell. Now, how did she get out?

She walked carefully, following the tunnel. After about five minutes, the tunnel ran into a bigger passage, which led to three other tunnels. There was no indication as to which way to go.

Ysabel sat down on a rock and pushed her hair out of her eyes. Which way? There were over three hundred kilometers of catacombs under Paris. She drew a deep breath and stood up. At least she was free. If she were going to die, she'd rather die looking for a way out than die in a cell. Ysabel bent down and mixed some dirt in a puddle of water. She marked a Y near the floor on the tunnel she'd taken. It was barely visible, but she could backtrack if she needed to do so. She shivered a bit as she made her way down the corridor. She prayed the flashlight had fresh batteries.

* * *

Harbinger and Smith loitered at the corner bistro where they were to meet the contact Con had found for them. "He'll show," Smith said as he drank the iced coffee he'd ordered.

"H, this is CCS."

Harbinger glanced over at Smith, who nodded that he'd heard the communication, too.

"Go ahead." He looked at Smith as he talked.

"Pierre made a call on the cell, but it was to a local bakery."

"An intermediary?" Smith asked.

"Unknown. We tapped into the cameras in the area as soon as we pinned the location. The phone call lasted thirty seconds."

"What was said?"

"He needed a delivery of baguettes. They

discussed the price, and Archambeau told them he'd have his assistant call to confirm. Nothing seemed out of the ordinary."

"Except a multi-millionaire calling for a catering arrangement," Smith said. "It was code."

"We thought so, too. I tapped into his switchboard for his business, which took a hot minute. They have some really good safeguards, but the comms aren't on fiber. If they were, we'd be screwed. His computer systems are, though, and man, is that security state of the art."

"You can determine if he calls out?"

"I can monitor all the calls, which I'm routing through a recording device and into a program I have that can isolate Pierre's voice. It'll alert me to any call he makes."

"Where did you get his voice?" Smith asked.

"A video of him speaking at the crypto summit held last year. He spoke about the sustainability of cryptocurrencies. It was more than enough to train my program."

Harbinger tapped Smith's foot with his. Smith glanced around and saw the man they were looking for. "We've got to go," Harbinger said.

"CCS clear." The woman was gone.

Harbinger turned to look at the guy, and at his

attention, the man moved over to their table. "Are you the ones looking for a private tour guide?"

"We are," Harbinger said as he stood. "I believe you require our requested itinerary?" He handed the man an envelope.

The gentleman opened the envelope and peeked in at the stack of high-denomination euros. "Shall we?"

The man seemed a bit jittery until they left the area. "So, you're not the police?" the man asked as they walked down the sidewalk. "If you were, you'd have arrested me before we left the area in which you'd taken a position. So, what are you looking for?" He stopped and crossed his arms, looking at Smith. "You're going to have a hard time in the tunnels. They were made by people shorter than the modern human."

Smith shrugged. "I'll be fine."

"We're looking for a place where a person could be held."

The man shifted his gaze to Harbinger before taking the envelope out of his pocket and handed it back to him. "I'm not into that type of thing."

"We're looking for a woman we believe is being held against her will in the tunnels," Smith said quietly.

"Damn." The man shoved the envelope back into his pocket. "I'm Matt."

"H."

"Smith."

The man shook their hands. "Okay. You'll need to look in the areas that aren't mapped. We have extensive mapping of the areas closed to the public, an amphitheater, and even a bar down there. There are crystal clear aquafers where people go scuba diving. Of the three hundred kilometers, we have about half the distance mapped, and it isn't uncommon to see other people below. So, whoever has your woman would want to stay clear of our areas." The man rubbed his face. "I know a guy making it his personal goal to map the outlying areas. Let me make a call and see if he can meet us."

Harbinger reached out and stopped the man from turning away. "Her life depends on us finding her. Don't fuck around on us."

Matt frowned. "I'm not planning on it. I'm trying to help." When Harbinger let go of his arm, Matt turned and walked off about twenty feet before making his call. He came back to them. "He can meet us. Come with me."

Harbinger and Smith followed the man to an

older-looking apartment building. They entered it and went down to the basement. From there, Matt removed a piece of paneling and took three flashlights from a bucket in the corner of the room. He also grabbed a package of batteries for the lights. "Take a water." The man nodded to a sealed case of water. Harbinger grabbed one, and so did Smith, but only after giving one to Matt. The guy nodded to the opening. "This is one of the many that will take us down. Follow me."

The passage was narrow, and when he looked back to check, Smith walked more sideways than straight and would have one hell of a backache because of the bent-over hunch he had going on, but they made good time. Harbinger placed a small dot on the limestone at each turn. They would reflect light and mark their way back. He didn't trust the man leading. It wasn't anything against Matt, just a fact of life. Trusting the wrong people could get you killed. Harbinger knew that for a fact. That was what happened to his sister and her friend. They'd trusted a man and were raped and murdered for it. The man who did it was tried and let off on a technicality. A technicality. The DA chose not to retry the case because, without the evidence that couldn't be admitted, they didn't feel the case was strong enough.

Harbinger knew what to do about that, and it was through his actions Demos found him. He wasn't one to dwell in the past. *Right.* Well, he hadn't been until Ysabel walked out of his life.

He peeled off a dot and slapped it on the tunnel wall as they turned again.

His sister, Kelly, and her best friend, Cathy, were in college when it happened. He attended the same college but had his own apartment and studied theater, where Kelly and Cathy pursued business as their major. He'd always wanted to be an actor, and now, well, he acted every day, and the world was his stage. The teaching assistant who'd offered his sister and her best friend a ride to a party had drugged their drinks, raped, killed, and mutilated them. Harbinger remembered the day he was finally allowed to see the crime scene photos. His mother looked at the pictures for two seconds and vomited. His father seemed to wither in on himself, and Harbinger became the one to drive the family's need for justice. His mom turned to alcohol, and his father turned inward. He met with the prosecutors, who promised him they had the evidence to convict the man. Until the defense submitted a break in the chain of evidence. The bastard's DNA was not admissible. It was what tied him to the rapes and the murders because there was no other physical evidence.

Two weeks after the dismissal of all charges, Harbinger began his first official performance. He used the makeup techniques he'd learned and changed his appearance and height. Now, looking back, the change wasn't enough, but he didn't know then what he knew now. He walked to the man's apartment and knocked on the door. When the TA opened the door, Harbinger lifted the gun he'd purchased on a street corner from a known drug dealer and fired. One through the brain. It was too good for the bastard. He dropped the gun, which he'd ensured didn't have any print or trace evidence on it. Harbinger walked down the stairs and didn't look at the other tenants who rushed out of their apartments to see what had happened. He walked across town, dropping his wig and stripping out of the clothes he wore on top of his own clothes. Each item found a home with a homeless person or in a dumpster. He went into a bar and had a drink, making sure the bartender saw him and could identify him. He waited for an hour and then hailed a cab back to campus and his apartment.

The police arrived two days later. The investigator demanded to know where he was the evening of the murder. Harbinger remembered the feeling of absolute freedom when he crossed his arms and requested a lawyer. They had nothing on him. He knew it, and he wasn't going to talk to the investigator. They arrested him, which he'd expected. It was a tactic he'd seen used many times on the true crime shows he watched. They could hold him for twenty-four hours without charging him.

He was roused from a fitful sleep when the officer let a man wearing a finely tailored suit into his cell.

"Horatio Langdon?"

Harbinger sat up and stared at the man. "Call me H." He hated the family name, even though he was currently Horatio Langdon the Seventh."

"My name is Demos. I'm here to make you an offer."

He leaned back against the wall of the cell. "I'm not talking without my lawyer present."

"Good, then listen because I won't repeat myself. You killed Larry Finch. I can prove it." Demos pulled photos out of his pocket. They showed him walking away from the bastard's apartment and showed each time he peeled off a layer of clothing. It showed him entering the club, and the timestamp was accurate. Then it showed him hailing a cab at the correct time, too. Demos tapped the time and date stamps to make sure Harbinger took note of them. "Excellent idea, poor execution."

The certainty he would get away with his vengeance disappeared as Demos picked up each picture in sequence. "That being said, I'm impressed with the attempt. I'm offering you one chance to get out of this mess. I know why you killed him. I understand the need for vengeance. My question for you is, could you do it again?"

Harbinger looked around the cell. Could he speak freely? Demos smiled. "I'm not a lawyer or a cop, nor am I someone who would testify in a court of law. You may speak freely."

Leaning forward, Harbinger stared at the distinguished man across from him. "I could if the bastard did what he did to my sister and her best friend. People like that don't deserve to be on this planet."

A twitch of Demos' lip was the only indication he'd said the right thing. "I'm in a position to offer you an opportunity to put this behind you and to hunt bastards like the man who slaughtered your sister and her friend. You would leave this life, and you could never come back. You will be tested to ensure my evaluation of your ability is correct. If it is, you will join an elite organization that eliminates the monsters of this world that the court system can't or won't."

"My parents?" They were a mess, and if they found

out he'd killed that bastard, they probably wouldn't survive.

"Will be taken care of. Your mother needs inpatient alcoholic rehabilitation treatment, and your father needs help also, but in a psychiatric hospital. Our company will see to it they're afforded every opportunity to heal and move on."

"Will they be told I'm dead?"

"No, and you can check on them. Coming back here isn't an option. Contacting anyone but your parents isn't an option. You will walk away tonight and forget everyone you've ever known."

Harbinger stared at the man. "I accept."

"Follow me."

Demos stood up, and Harbinger followed him out of the jail. The jailor was asleep and another in a guard uniform followed them out of the jail. Harbinger glanced up at the cameras. "They're on a loop and not recording us," the guard said, noticing the direction of his gaze. Another guard opened the door to the outside and followed them out. All four men got into a blacked-out SUV and drove out of the compound, through the guarded entrance, and onto the access road. That was the beginning of Harbinger's new life. He'd checked on his parents. They were doing well, and he talked to them three or four times a year. They had a contact number, and should they need him, Guardian would let him know.

Harbinger slapped another dot on a turn and almost ran into Matt when he stopped. "Careful here, we need to go around the aquafer." Matt's light illuminated the water in front of them. "Louis will be on the other side about a kilometer farther."

CHAPTER 9

sabel stared at the water. The reflection of the pool stretched as far as the light of her torch illuminated. She slowly walked forward. Resting was the priority at the moment. There was no way to gauge how far she'd come to reach that point. Finding a way across the water would be a worry ... after she rested. She tried to ward off the chill of the subterranean lake by wrapping her arms around her legs and resting her head on her knees.

The silence of the cavern was a blessing and a curse. It was a blessing because she didn't have to waste the light to see what animal or insect was making the noise, and a curse because she'd blindly hoped that, at some point, she'd find people or a way out. Neither had been realized.

The positive was that no one followed her. So, the people who wanted her captive either didn't know she'd escaped, or they couldn't find her. Again, a good and a bad thing. If people searching for her couldn't find her, how could she hope to find a way out? Her knees were scraped from falling on the slick limestone. She'd bumped her head several times because she'd been looking down to watch where her feet were going. Her shoulders were scratched from some of the tight passages, and she was physically exhausted.

She wanted to lie down and cry, but that would solve nothing. Something inside her told her not to give up, and she wouldn't as long as she had light. And after that, she'd feel her way forward if she had to do so. Ysabel shivered and hugged her arms. She should have thought of grabbing her shirt off the lamp and taking a bottle of water, but escaping was the priority. So, now, she stood tired, cold, and thirsty. The water in the cavern was enticing, but she'd heard stories of people getting very sick from water that wasn't purified. She'd wait before risking that desperate move.

Her father would have someone looking for

her. She knew he'd try to find her, but how would he know she was underground in Paris when she'd been taken from Corsica? She spun the ring her mother had given to her with her thumbnail. It had an ugly, large, black stone, but it was the one thing of her mother's that she had. The envelope she'd given to her father. He'd insisted she must have dropped some of the documents, but she hadn't, and she was sure of it. The ring she kept as her own. Her father wouldn't be happy if he knew her mother had forgotten the documents but included a ring. It was cheap costume jewelry, the kind of which her father would frown upon.

She should have another ring on that finger. The beautiful square diamond surrounded by emeralds Heath had given her. She'd been so happy. So in love. That night was a dream. He'd arranged a private dinner for them at the Eiffel Tower. The warm summer air carried the sounds of the city below. When he dropped to one knee, she'd been confused at first. Then, oh dear God, the *words* he said. The love in his eyes. Heath asked her to be his wife, to hold his heart forever, and to allow him to cherish her for the rest of her life.

She'd sunk to her knees in front of him and said yes. It was the most perfect moment. But less than a week later, she tore their love apart and fled to Corsica. No matter how much she'd suffered from that moment at the ball, Heath had to have suffered more. She'd never met a kinder or more gentle-mannered man. Her father was right. Protecting him from the danger of her mother's alleged theft of the information was the right thing to do.

Ysabel kicked something, and she flashed the light in the direction of the noise. It was an aluminum can. She scanned the area. There another and another. People came here. She picked up the can. It was clean; it hadn't been long since they'd been in the area. She almost cried in relief. She could wait. She could wait, and someone would come. She found a flat piece of rock and sat down. How long could she wait? How long would it take? Still, this was her best chance of finding someone to help her out of this maze.

TIME LAPSED into naps and bouts of shivering. She was so thirsty and so cold. As she faded into sleep again, the sound of voices across the lake brought her head up. She blinked in the complete darkness and patted the ground for her flashlight. Had she been dreaming? Had she fallen asleep? She held her breath and searched the darkness. There. A light. The sound of male voices.

Ysabel stood up and turned on her flashlight, waving it back and forth. "Help! Please, help me!" Her throat was so dry she could barely speak, but she waved the light for all she was worth.

Three lights pointed in her direction. "Yes! Here! Help me!"

"Ysabel?" The call came from the other side of the water.

Her heart jumped into her throat at the familiar voice. "*Heath?* Heath! I'm here!"

She heard some heated words, and then there was a splash in the water. Two lights started to skirt the side of the wall, but Ysabel focused on the man swimming toward her. She held the light on him and knew in her heart it was Heath. She sank to her knees, tears streaming as she waited. He made it across the water with long, strong strokes. Standing, he ran out of the water and dropped in front of her. The flashlight bounced on the ground as he held her face and stared down at her. "Are you all right?"

"I am now. Heath, they put me in a cell. I hit a

man over the head and locked him in the cell, then I left. I walked forever. How did you get here? How did you know I was here?" Ysabel knew she was babbling and had no idea if he understood a word she said, but the feel of his arms around her was more than enough. Her words dissolved into tears, and his hushed words of comfort in her ear made her cry harder. "I love you. I love you so much, I didn't want to do it. I didn't want to hurt you."

* * *

Harbinger held the woman he loved more than his life in his arms. Someone would pay for her tears and the landscape of bruises covering her. He whispered in her ear as he gauged where Smith and their guide were.

Ysabel grabbed his wet shirt and pulled away. "I love you."

He pushed her hair away from her face. "I know. I know." He wrapped her in his arms and held her close to his heart. He'd never let her go again. "You're safe now."

"Are you ready?" Smith said from somewhere near him. He and Matt had taken the long way, using the small path that went around the lake. Harbinger couldn't wait that long, so he dove in.

He looked up. "Yes, we need to get to the surface ASAP." He took back his cell phone and earpiece from Smith.

"There are several exits."

"No, wait." Ysabel sniffed. "I hit a man in the head with a rock. He's in the cell where I was held. I don't know how badly I hurt him."

"We'll never find it," Matt said. "These tunnels here aren't marked or mapped."

"I marked my way so I could find my way back if I couldn't go farther. I made a small Y near the floor at each turn."

"Matt, we'll take them up and find this man." Smith stood at his full height and crossed his arms, daring the man to counter his decision.

"Might cost you a bit more," Matt said.

"Money is not an issue." Smith pulled out his wallet and handed the man a solid inch stack of Euros.

"Then, my friend, you have a guide for life." Matt shoved the money into his back pocket. "This way."

Harbinger helped Ysabel to stand. "May I?"

Smith asked as he shrugged off his long-sleeved shirt and handed it to Ysabel.

Harbinger nodded at his friend in a silent thank you for the clothing. His wet clothes wouldn't have been much help to her. He helped Ysabel into the fabric. She looked up at Smith. "Thank you."

"My pleasure," Smith said and motioned toward Matt.

"Right this way." Matt led them with Harbinger and Ysabel in the middle and Smith in the rear. He knew the big guy would have his weapon drawn, especially after what Ysabel had told them. Harbinger's weapon was with Smith, too. He'd get it back before they hit the street above.

"How did you find me?" Ysabel asked him again.

"My company was able to assess where you were from the photograph your father had received."

"We need to tell him I'm all right. He must be going crazy with worry."

He made some noise of agreement as he guided her around a limestone outcropping. It took ten minutes to make it to an accessway. Matt shone a light up the small crevice. Smith looked at Matt and then at the crevice. "Tell me there's a larger access point somewhere?"

"Yes, farther up this way, but I assumed you wanted her out of here as quickly as possible."

"I'll be right back down. It won't take longer than five minutes to get them to the top." Matt handed Smith all the money he'd been given, including the envelope he was given earlier. "To prove my intent is pure. Besides, if we don't meet Louis, he'll never work with me again, and I won't risk that."

Matt took the lead, and Harbinger shook Smith's hand. "I'll let Val know what's going on."

Smith made a face. "She'll be overjoyed."

Harbinger smiled at his friend, who was absolutely correct. The assassin wouldn't be happy. Harbinger helped Ysabel into the crevice, barely managing to squeeze himself through the opening. Several yards ahead, it widened, and he was able to breathe easier. Matt was true to his word. They emerged in a shack in the garden of some old house. "If you ever need a guide, feel free to contact me again." Matt touched his head with two fingers and headed back down.

Ysabel shook. She was probably crashing from

the adrenaline she'd existed on in the tunnels. "What do we do now?"

Holding up a finger, Harbinger tapped his earpiece. "Sunset Operative Seventeen, I need immediate pickup at my geotag."

"I copy. Status?"

"I have Ysabel Archambeau. Sunset Operative Thirteen Bravo is still below with the guide looking for the cell and one injured target."

"Affirmative. Are you secure?"

"Affirmative," Harbinger said as he glanced out the dirty window of the shack. "Standing by for transport."

"To what location?" the operator asked.

"Sunset Operative Thirteen's location. My building is being watched."

"I copy. Operator Two-Seven-Four is standing by."

He glanced at Ysabel, who frowned at him and asked, "Who are you talking to?"

"My company." He tapped his earpiece and moved so she could see it.

"You said you were a troubleshooter. I assumed IT or management. It isn't so, is it?"

Harbinger shook his head. "Security."

Isabel closed her eyes and shook her head. "I

should've known that. I should've known you could take care of you and me. Why did I listen to him?"

"Your father? I don't know. I assume you thought he was doing what was right. But I do question what happened."

Ysabel sat down on a wooden box. "Why?" She looked up at him. "Tell me, Heath. Tell me what you're thinking. No more secrets between us, please."

Harbinger kneeled in front of her. "I never told you a lie."

Ysabel sighed and dropped her head into her hands. "This, I believe. Why don't you trust my father?"

"Call it gut instinct."

"You're right there." Con's voice was in his ear. "Daddo is in on the game. He just got a call on the cloned cell phone that the order for the bread he wanted had gone missing. I'm thinking they know she's gone from the cell."

Harbinger jerked to look at the opening to the catacombs. "Smith is still down there."

Con muttered some choice swear words. "Then he better be careful."

"He will be." Val's voice came over the comms.

"He's got great instincts, and he's more intelligent than anyone underground; that's for sure."

"What are they saying?" Ysabel asked.

"Your father received a call just now telling him you were no longer in the cell." Harbinger wasn't going to pull any punches. She had to know the truth.

"No." She dropped her head into her hands. "No ... he knew?" She looked up at him. "But why? My God, why would he do this?"

"He was the only one who knew you were in Corsica," Harbinger stated.

She nodded. "Yes."

"Double that yes. That was confirmed by Giovanni and Tango Team. We just got the call," Jewell King chirped into the conversation. "The people guarding her in Corsica were told to take a walk by their bosses. They did, and she was gone when they returned."

Harbinger looked at her. "Your father could've been a party to the kidnapping from Corsica."

Ysabel's shaking grew worse. He pulled her into his arms, and she dropped her head against his chest. He held her a bit tighter, wishing none of it was happening to her but dealing with the fact it was.

"My question is, what changed to make him bring her back to Paris, and why did he come to search you out?" That was Fury. Well, hell, everyone was in on the conversation, weren't they?

Ysabel sniffed back silent tears. "I don't understand any of this."

"Neither do I. But we don't need to understand anything at the moment. I'm taking you somewhere safe, and then we'll figure out the next move." Ysabel nodded her head against him in agreement.

"The next move is grabbing Pierre and pulling out his toenails one by one until he tells us what the hell is going on," Fury growled.

"Not until we get approval from my counterpart in the French government. We don't want an international incident," Archangel chastised Fury.

Harbinger held Ysabel against him as the discussion continued. She shook her head. "Why? Why would he do this? Was it the man my mother was married to? Did he make my father do this?"

"I wish I knew," Harbinger whispered against her hair.

"H, your car is out front," Con said. "Out the door of the shack, take a right around the house, and it's the black limo."

"Copy." He tipped Ysabel's head back by placing his finger under her chin. "I have never lied to you. I never will. Any omission of my job's requirements was dictated because of security. If you ever needed to know, I would've told you. I will keep you safe. Do you trust me?"

Ysabel stared up at him. "With my life."

He bent down and kissed the woman he loved. A mere brush of his lips because they didn't have time to rediscover each other.

"Aw, that's so sweet." Jewell sighed into the comms.

He took Ysabel's hand, and together, they moved around the house and into the waiting car. Harbinger pulled her into him. Thank God, they'd found her. It was truly finding a needle in a haystack. He had no idea how expansive the tunnel system was. Knowing that now, it was a perfect place for a criminal element to operate. He rubbed her back and held her as the car moved through the residential area and into the main traffic heading toward the 16th Arrondissement and safety.

CHAPTER 10

Con stared at the camera, watching the man who was watching traffic in front of the building.

"Who do you think he's waiting for?" Jewell asked.

"I don't have a clue," Fury answered. "Who would try to get to H?"

"Besides Archambeau? Maybe they're watching for someone who wants to find Ysabel?" Jewell mused.

"Like who? The mother? She was the one who warned her daughter." Fury sounded contemplative, too.

Jewell made a dismissive sound. "She's dead,

right? And she only warned Ysabel about Abrasha, right?"

Fury sighed. "I haven't seen the documents. I can't make that assumption, but that is what Harbinger said."

Con tapped his fingers on the desktop. "So, assuming the documents held information on AM, why would they target this building?"

"Was Ysabel staying with H? I mean, were they living together? They were close before she broke things off," Jewell asked.

"No clue," Con said.

"Go look in his closet," Fury snapped.

"Dude, you want me to invade the privacy of an elite assassin, who, by the way, can change his appearance to look like someone totally different. That is so not cool." Con stood up and made his way out of the comm room.

"Just fucking do it," Fury barked.

"I am. Shit, chill out," Con snapped back. "Bossy asshole."

Jewell sighed, "Boys, do I need to tell your moms?"

God, no. He rolled his eyes as he wandered down the hall and peeked into a door. Nope. Linen storage. He kept going and opened another. A massive room with a king-sized bed and an ensuite bathroom. Crossing the hall, he opened another door. There were clothes, both male and female. "Female clothing," Con said and headed into the bathroom. He opened several cabinets. "Perfume, makeup, jewelry. Yep, she was living here or staying over regularly."

"Could the mother be alive?" Jewell asked. "Think about it. We have a death certificate, but do we know for a fact she's dead?"

"Banshee is in Switzerland," Fury said. "Let me get him to do some looking around. There have to be records from a funeral home or a person who signed the death certificate. Dead bodies don't usually go unnoticed." Fury sighed. "Other than the mother, who would want to get to Harbinger, and why?"

"Ysabel," Con said.

"But if her father put her into the catacombs and is part of this mess ..." Jewell let the statement trail.

"Shit, just suppose ... What if the father didn't, and he actually has people trying to find her down there like we do?" Fury brought up an interesting point.

Con doubted that premise, though. "Dude,

then who told the Corsican Mafia to stand down?"

"Someone with more pull with the boss than Archambeau," Fury replied.

"Like?" Con could see what the asshole was talking about now, but damn, what a double-cross on Ysabel's father.

"Abrasha," Jewell supplied. "By all accounts, he has the Russian Mafia wrapped around his finger. If one faction reached out to the other and requested a favor? That's a plausible scenario."

Fury made a sound of agreement. "I'll reach out to our resident Mafia specialist and see if they can pull some strings."

"Phoenix?" Jewell snorted. "I think he burned all his bridges. Literally."

Fury gave that eerie, evil laugh of his. "True, but I wasn't thinking about him. I was thinking of Taty. She still has connections in the Russian Mafia. Her contemporaries have risen since she's gone silent, but she keeps tabs on several people."

Con sat in one of the living room chairs and kicked his feet up on the fancy-looking coffee table. The golden cat that had fled from the kitchen sat on the sofa across from him and stared at him suspiciously. Con stared back at it and asked, "So, what does she do? Ask if Abrasha has plans on killing his daughter?"

"No, asshole, she asks if Abrasha is calling in favors and from whom. They'd never talk about anything concrete," Fury snapped at him.

"So sorry, my Mafia etiquette is lacking. What do you want us to do?" He would get twitchy if he didn't have a project. He might figure out how to make Fury's private cell phone play obnoxious music or something. A smirk plastered itself across his face. Or something.

"Get Harbinger everything you can on Pierre Archambeau. Flack and CCS are following Molchalin and his other daughter's trail. I want to know what color underwear he's wearing. But that's your side gig. Jewell, your organization's primary mission is to monitor what's going on with Archambeau's crypto heist. Counter the theft if necessary and reroute the crypto after it's transferred."

"He has fiber, and the computer systems are not linked," Jewell interjected.

"Would he have thieves working out of his supposedly legit business? If someone tracked the access back to him …" Fury asked.

Con leaned forward. "Jewell, we can see what

property he owns and which we'd pick if we were setting up a covert operation."

"That's right. And we could cross reference with any work done such as cable installation or new power requirements. They'd need supercomputer access, so we'd also need to check with the government of France to see if they've greenlighted the sale of any to private entities." Jewell was typing as Con headed back through the house.

He started jogging to get to his system faster. "You take the government. I've got the property records, and I'll start working on Archambeau. I'm going to see what property Abrasha has in Paris, too, just in case."

"Good call. Check under all their shell companies and both of AM's daughters' names. Bad people don't care if their kids get caught in shit," Jewell told him.

"Yep. Talk later." His mind was racing with ideas and ways to circumvent the tech the guy must have to break into those fobs. God, he loved a challenge.

"Got it. Clear," Jewell said.

"And I'm clear if anyone cares." Fury sighed and hung up. Con barked out a laugh. The asshole was kind of comical for a grumpy, old, curmudgeonly assassin.

CHAPTER 11

Shivering uncontrollably, Ysabel let Heath help her up the stairs to his friend's apartment. He didn't have to knock before a beautiful woman opened the door and stood aside, letting them in.

"We need to get her warm," Heath said as he held her.

"The shower." The woman led them through a beautifully appointed flat and into a bedroom with a large marble-lined shower. "I'll get the towels in the warmer and put them outside the door. I'll have food whenever you're ready to come out. Hopefully, Smith will be home by then."

"He's the one who gave me this?" Ysabel touched the fine cotton shirt she was wearing.

The woman smiled. "Yes, he's my husband."

"He's going to be all right," Heath told her. "He's too damn smart to be caught short."

"Which is what I told you. I'm not worried, just pissed I couldn't be there to kick some ass, too. I want to be with him, but I'm sure you understand." Val smiled sadly and nodded to the shower. "Get her warm. I'll call Con and get some clothes for you, H."

"Ysabel has clothes at my place," Heath called after her.

Val turned around. "I'll get her some of her clothes, too. I'll send a messenger service over to pick them up. Feel free to use anything in the bathroom or bedroom. I'll leave everything outside the bedroom door."

Ysabel watched the beautiful woman shut the door behind her. "She's nice and so beautiful."

"Beautiful on the inside as well as the out. She's a good friend." Heath chuckled. "Come on. We need to get you warm." He walked with her into the bathroom, and she gasped when she saw herself in the mirror. "My God." She walked over and stared at her reflection. Bruises mottled her face and under her eye. There was fresh blood from where she'd slammed her head into the low stone ceiling of the caverns while trying to escape. Her hair was nothing but knots and snarls, and she was filthy. Dirt smeared under her eyes where tears had formed clean streaks. Her body, arms, and hands were covered in dirt, and the filth under her broken fingernails showed when she'd tried to dig and pry herself out of that damn cell.

"A shower will help," Heath said, guiding her back to the shower he'd turned on. Ysabel stepped out of her filthy slacks and panties and dropped the huge, borrowed shirt and her bra. She'd been naked in front of Heath so many times there was no reason to be bashful. Stepping under the water, she let the warmth flow over her.

She knew Heath entered the shower with her and leaned into him when she felt his strong arms band around her. There, under the fall of water, Ysabel leaned into the man she loved and let herself sob. The regret, the pain of her father's treachery, and the fact that Heath had yet to say he loved her. Had she ruined everything? Had she lost her chance at a life with him?

She realized he was rocking with her under the spray of the shower's water. "I'm so sorry." Her voice trembled with the weight of her words and regret she couldn't bear any longer.

"You tore my heart out." His hoarse whisper made her cry harder. She could feel the hurt and damage consume the air around them like a tsunami, brutal, crushing, and deadly.

His confession made her tears fall faster, each pushing into a ripple that grew wider and wider. Words she never should have uttered had wounded them both horribly. "I know. I don't know how to make it right."

He continued to hold her in a gentle embrace and rock with her from side to side in a rhythmic dance that needed no music. "You don't need to make it right. I couldn't stop loving you. I never did. I never would. God knows I tried to forget, to move on, but I couldn't. You're the living part of my soul. I only existed without you; I didn't *live*."

She tightened her grip around his waist and held onto him as if he were her lifeline. "I love you, Heath." Her whispered words were barely spoken, but their weight resonated with truth and honesty.

"I know," he whispered. Small words that held forgiveness, understanding, and acceptance. She heard them and let them soak in, down to the deepest pain and most desolate places. To her heart that had withered and decayed without him.

He unwrapped one arm, and she felt him work

the lightly scented soap up and down her back. When she stopped crying, he kissed her lips gently and turned her around. Heath washed her body with gentle hands, tenderly cleaning the large bruises on her legs and shoulders. She leaned back so he could shampoo her hair. The delicate floral fragrance perfumed the steam. He conditioned her hair, and while he let it work, he carefully washed her face, kissing each bruise as he uncovered it.

After rinsing out her hair, he turned off the water. Then he wrapped her in a huge bath sheet and set her at the vanity where he'd placed his phone and earpiece. Heath secured a towel around his waist and then worked a comb through her hair. She closed her eyes as he carefully fixed the tangles. As he worked, her mind floated back to what he'd said earlier. "What makes you think my father did this?"

Heath didn't answer right away. "There are usually three things that cause people to act out of character. Money, love, or power. Which caused your father to act as he did is unknown."

She sighed. "He has money, he has power, and I don't believe he's truly loved me or anyone as much as I wanted him to. I want to talk to him. To ask him why."

When Heath stopped combing her hair momentarily, she opened her eyes, catching his gaze in the mirror as he spoke. "I'll make sure you have that opportunity to speak to him, but please wait for me to arrange it. We don't know who or what is involved with this situation, and there's more going on than you know. More than I can tell you without permission from my superiors. I know you want answers, and so do I, but right now, we can't make a move without compromising your position. You're safe here. Smith and Val will ensure that, and there are very few I trust completely. They are two people who I do."

"My mother's message caused so much trouble." She glanced down at the ring on her finger. "Why?"

Heath put the comb down and sat beside her on the bench. "Where did you get that?"

"The ring?" she asked as he looked at it and nodded.

"My mom. It was in the envelope." She pulled it off and handed it to him. "My father would tell me to throw it away if he knew she gave it to me. It's inexpensive. He detests cheap things."

She watched as Heath turned on a light by the mirror and leaned in, examining the ring. "You told no one you had this, that it was in the envelope?"

She shook her head. "I didn't see a reason to tell anyone. As I said, it isn't expensive. Why?"

Heath turned to her. "Because I think I found the documents she claimed to have sent you."

Ysabel frowned. "What? Where?"

"In the stone." Heath pointed to the smoky grayish-black stone. "Entire books can be inscribed on a medium smaller than this."

"What do you think is on it?" She stared at the ring, trying to see what he saw. "Wait, how can you see it? I don't see anything. Are you sure?"

"See here when I hold it up to the light, that thin straight line going through the stone, that could be the flat, where the inscription is written. I may be way off here. It could be nothing, or ..."

"Or it could be everything she said it would be," Ysabel whispered.

"What exactly did she say was included in the documents?" Heath put the ring on the vanity and turned to her.

"Ah, I can't remember the exact words. My father has the letter now, but she told me about giving birth to me in the States and included my original birth certificate. It was old and folded in a small square, yellowed on the outside folds like it had been tucked somewhere for a long time. Then she said she'd realized in the past ten years or so what Abrasha was doing. Abrasha is the name of my real father. She went back to him after she gave birth to me." Ysabel sighed and dropped her eyes. "I can understand that type of love. I'd do anything to get back to you."

Heath pushed her damp hair behind her ear. "I'd never ask you to give up our baby."

Ysabel blinked and looked up at him. "How did you know that? How did you know he asked her to abort me? I didn't tell you that."

"Your father did when he was here asking for my help."

Ysabel frowned. "Why would he do that?"

"He thought I was a government agent." Heath put his forehead against hers.

"Why?" She tried to laugh, but it came out more like a sob.

"As a security specialist, I saw his private investigators. I easily avoided them, so he thought that made me a spy."

Ysabel did manage to laugh at that. "You? A spy?"

"Right? Who would believe that? What did your mom say about the documents?"

She sighed and closed her eyes, her body suddenly very heavy. "That there was enough information to ruin him." She yawned and folded against him. "I'm sorry, I'm so tired."

"You're crashing. It's normal. Do you want to eat something before you go to sleep?"

She barely shook her head. The effort seemed to cost more energy than she had.

Heath gathered her into his arms, and she floated to sleep, warm and safe in his embrace.

CHAPTER 12

In bed, Harbinger held her longer than he should have. Having her in his arms fed something so deep in his soul he couldn't let her go for over an hour. He hadn't lied to her; he'd only existed in the slimmest margins of life when she was gone. His love for her surpassed anything he'd ever known.

The first time they'd made love, he'd felt the shift. The day he told her he loved her, and she admitted to the same feeling, the change in him had been immediate, intense, epic in every way. He was a different person with her by his side. Without her, he was a shell. After he'd exhausted his ways to find her, he'd become hollow. His communications with his team had dropped to the bare minimum to keep them out of his life. He let his training go. He drank too much and walked the streets of Paris at night looking for a fight. He'd found more than one. He was a flaming aircraft en route to a crash landing. But Demos had showed up at his door because Smoke was worried about him.

"What in the hell are you doing, boy?" Demos pushed his way into the apartment. "God, it stinks in here." He walked to the window and opened it. "Go take a shower, then we're going to have a moment."

"No, I'm good."

"Like hell you are." Demos sat down on the couch, and Spike jumped up to inspect the newcomer.

"Why are you here?" Harbinger flopped into the chair across from Demos.

"Smoke called me. You've had long enough. Time to find a way to shake off what happened and get your ass back to the man you are. This is a defining moment, boy. This is where you suck it up and either deal with what happened or bury it so far down you'll bleed if you think about it again."

"I'm already bleeding."

"Because you have it in your hand, and you keep searching for an answer. Sometimes in life there aren't

any answers. Love is amazing, and it sucks, too. You got the suckage end right now. Deal. With. It."

"Thanks for the support."

"You've had support for the last how many months? This stops, or you're out."

Harbinger's gut clenched, and he blinked in confusion. Out? Out meant out of Guardian. Out of the team. Out of his fucking purpose in life. "Out?"

"You heard me. You're an elite assassin. You got your ass kicked by a woman you loved. It happens. You've had time to deal with it on your own. Either pick yourself up and move forward with help from our shrinks, or you're out."

Harbinger rubbed his face. Damn, had it come to that? He looked around his apartment. The filth had built layer upon layer because he didn't want his housekeeper to come inside. She left his groceries at the doorstep every week. He swallowed hard. "Define out."

"I don't have to. You know what out means. If you have any hope of meeting that woman in the future or maybe having another reason to fall in love, you need to get your shit in order. Now, go take a shower and think about the answer. Either yes, you're in, or no, you're out. I won't ask again."

Harbinger stood up. "I'm in." He walked to the shower and drew a deep breath. The line had been drawn. He took off his clothes and turned on the water. Getting into the shower, he grabbed the bar of soap and said out loud, "Maybe that's what you needed all along. Someone to come kick your ass out of this funk."

As he looked down at her sleeping beside him, he thanked God she was in his arms and alive. All those empty places were filled once again. Harbinger leaned down and kissed her forehead before sliding out of the bed. He opened the bedroom door, grabbed the bag sitting beside it, and got dressed. He placed Ysabel's clothes on the chair beside the bed before taking one more look at the woman he loved, and then he headed out to find Val.

Val glanced over at him from where she sat in the front room. "Is she okay?"

"Yeah, thanks. She's sleeping." Harbinger glanced around the room. "Smith?"

"I haven't heard from him. Neither has Guardian." Val's foot tapped the air restlessly. "She has some of the same features as Smith. The eyebrows and cheekbones."

"She does now that I think about it. Look, I'm not leaving him down there alone. I'm going back down." Harbinger turned around to find his boots, locating them by the door.

"No, you don't know where he is. He's a smart man. He's a fighter," Val said, probably as much to reassure herself as him.

"I've seen what he's capable of, true." Harbinger sat down on the couch with his boots. "That message he sent from that train when I was in Mongolia to meet the two of you, that was … loud."

Val smiled sadly before leaning forward and looking directly at him. "I don't know why, but I've got this feeling something's wrong."

Harbinger could see the worry in her eyes. He knew *that* fear and didn't want his friend to suffer from it. "I'll go back down. I know where we came up. Call Con and see if he can get another guide. If not, I'll mark my way."

Val stood up. "And if he comes out while you're down there?"

"Then we know he's safe. I'll mark time and come back up every three hours." Harbinger lifted one of his wet boots to put it on.

"He should be okay …" Val let the thought trail off. "Wait." Val froze and reached for her ear. Her eyes widened. "Go ahead." She jumped, then snapped, "Where? How bad? I'm heading there now. Yeah, like I care."

"What is it?" Harbinger had taken out his earpiece before stepping into the shower. He wanted his time with Ysabel to be private.

"Smith was shot. He's on the way to the hospital." Val jogged through the house and grabbed her purse. Shoving her hand in, she came out with an automatic. She slid the slide back, checked the chamber, and dropped it back into her purse. "I'll call from the hospital."

"Make sure you tell Con so he can erase any pictures of you." Harbinger stopped her. "Val, what's his status?"

"Con knows. Jewell said Smith was pissed, and he wanted me to stay here."

"He didn't think that would work, did he?" Harbinger asked as she marched to the door.

"Probably, he gets delusions sometimes. I'll call with updates." Val was gone in the next instant.

Harbinger dropped his head back and looked at the ceiling. Fuck, this day had been so damn long and full of surprises, good and bad. He made his way back down to the room he and Ysabel were using and quietly retrieved his earpiece. As he went into the kitchen, he activated the device.

"Harbinger to CCS." There were a few clicks on the device.

"Go," Jewell said.

"Any updates on Smith?"

"I'm getting pieces of information, but he has people around him and can't speak freely. The police were called because he was shot. The guide called the medics before he disappeared with someone named Louis. The medics called the cops. Smith is not happy."

"The police are on scene?"

Con joined the conversation. "No, they're responding to the hospital. Evidently, the injury took priority over any questioning."

"Do we have a medical status?"

"From what we're hearing, it isn't good," Con said. "My French is a bit rusty, but the medics are worried. An entry wound and no exit. They keep asking Smith how he was shot. The guy is smart. He said it was a mugging, but, dude, he's not being a good patient."

"Fuck," Harbinger hissed.

"I've got our Guardian doctor heading that way," Jewell said. "Hold on, the big guys are going to join the conversation."

"Status on Smith?" He recognized Archangel's

voice.

"Unknown. We believe a chest wound. No exit wound. We're getting piecemeal information. He's not alone."

"I'm fine," Smith snarled. "Probably a fucking ricochet."

"You don't know that," Harbinger snapped back. "Let them take care of you. Val is on her way."

"Fuck." Smith made a pathetic sound. "Is she pissed?"

"Oh, yeah," Harbinger answered him. "But not at you."

"Smith, we're putting you in listen mode. You let them do whatever they need. We'll handle the police." That was Fury.

"Good," he said. "The injury isn't bad. I can feel the bullet. Give me forceps, and I'll pull the fucker out."

"Listen mode on Smith's earpiece is engaged," Jewell reported.

"That fucker Pierre was involved in this." Fury's growl filled the connection.

"We don't know that," Archangel fired back.

"We would if you could get us permission to interrogate the son of a bitch," Fury returned the volley.

Archangel shut Fury down immediately. "Chill the fuck out. I have permission. H, you'll do the questioning."

"I can't leave Ysabel alone." Harbinger stared down the hallway to where she slept.

"Not asking you to. We have her safe now, and Smith will be released to the care of our doctor. Pierre's questioning can wait until tomorrow. Get him to come to you at your apartment. I want our team to hear what that bastard says, and from what you reported, they'll search and find your earpiece if you go to his facility."

Harbinger sat down and closed his eyes. Thankfully, he wouldn't have to put Ysabel in harm's way again today.

Archangel sighed. "Okay, bring me up to date."

"There have been no pictures of proof of life sent to the cell, so if Pierre asked for it, he should be getting worried." Con dropped that bit of information.

"Now that we have the switchboard monitored and his cell cloned, we'll know if he gets antsy. If he doesn't, it makes him look even guiltier," Jewell added.

"What about locations he could use to steal the

crypto?" Archangel inquired. "I don't see the connection between this theft and Ysabel's disappearance."

Con snorted, "Holding his daughter hostage is a big incentive, boss man."

"True, but Abrasha could go to people in Russia to have this crypto stolen. Some of the best hackers are in Russia and China. Why Pierre? Why that specific amount?"

The same questions had been going around in Harbinger's mind, but it also reminded him of something. "I have some new information."

"Go," Fury directed.

"I believe Ysabel had possession of the documents stolen from Abrasha all along. Her mother gave her a ring, which was in the document envelope. She didn't tell her father about the ring, afraid he'd tell her she couldn't have it."

"And?" Fury asked.

"And I can see a flat in the stone."

"Laser etching?" Jewell asked.

"I believe so," Harbinger replied. "We'll need some equipment, but, Con, you can find a way to see what's on the ring?"

"I can do that," Con readily agreed. "Probably.

I've never done it before, but it should be straightforward."

Jewell asked, "What do you need? I can ship it to you if necessary."

"I'll let you know. I'm learning about it now," Con answered, and Harbinger could hear the tapping of keyboards as they spoke.

Con came on the line again. "Hold on—Val's approaching the hospital. I need to scramble some cameras. I'll be back."

"Pierre holds information we need. Abrasha Molchalin is officially a person of interest for the Counsel because of his part in the failed invasion of Switzerland." Archangel continued, "H, the interrogation is yours. Get us that information."

"I understand." Harbinger would gladly shove bamboo shards under that fucker's fingernails if it would get them answers about who had taken Ysabel and why.

"Taty said her contacts in the Bratva refused to talk about Molchalin," Fury interjected. "So, that was no help."

"Jewell, keep me updated on Smith. Fury, call me now. Archangel is clear."

"Ouch, someone is going to get slapped." Con chuckled.

"Keep that shit up, and it'll be you," Fury growled. "The Rose is clear."

"You keep poking, my brother, and all the moms in the world won't be able to help you," Harbinger said.

"I know how far I can push him, but I'll back off. Give me some time to research how to read laser etching."

"You have until morning. I'll bring the ring over before I call Pierre and tell him to meet me." He hoped Smith wasn't injured too badly and Val would be back by then to watch Ysabel. Harbinger went into the kitchen, opened a bottle of Val's wine, and fixed himself something to eat. While he ate, he made a tray for Ysabel. Fruit, fresh baguette, cheese, sliced meat, and a tall glass of water. He put another wine glass on the tray and the bottle he'd opened. Glancing at his watch, he tapped his earpiece. "Con, any update on Smith?"

"Val said the doctors are concerned because the bullet at the surface is only a fraction of the slug. It could be a ricochet, or the bullet fractured, and parts of it went deeper. Smith is heading to radiology to ensure there isn't something else."

"All right. I'm going to listen mode." Harbinger didn't wait for a reply but tapped his earpiece three times and heard the distinct beep that meant he could listen when someone reached out to him, but no one would hear what he and Ysabel said to each other.

Harbinger balanced the tray in one hand and opened the bedroom door with the other. The sun was setting, and the room was cast in a golden hue. He put the tray on the bedside table and lay down facing Ysabel. He used the ends of her long black hair to tickle her nose. When she swiped at the hair, he did it again.

Her eyes popped open, and she shot into a sitting position.

"Hey, I didn't mean to scare you," Harbinger said, sitting up with her.

"Oh … Heath. I thought you were the rat." Ysabel buried her head in her hands.

"I'm sorry." He pulled her into him. "I didn't know."

"It was so big. I crammed rocks into the hole it used to leave." She shivered.

"You're safe now. I brought you some food." He wanted to divert her attention *and* get some food into her. She'd lost weight since he'd last seen her, and her naturally thin frame was gaunt.

Her stomach grumbled, and she clamped her

arms over it. He pulled her in and kissed her lightly. "Food." He twisted and picked up the tray, positioning it over her lap.

Ysabel grabbed the grapes and popped them into her mouth in rapid succession. "They didn't give me good food. Just junk."

"Junk food?"

She nodded and popped a section of orange into her mouth. When she finished, she pulled another section off the orange and explained, "Like the food you find in a gas station in the States. Do we know if the man I hit is all right?"

Harbinger shook his head. "Smith was shot while he was down in the tunnels. Our guide called an ambulance. Val is at the hospital with him."

Ysabel's hand slowly dropped, and she put the fruit down. "Because of me."

"No, because of whoever kidnapped you. Eat," he commanded. "None of this is your fault." Harbinger poured more wine into his glass and leaned back on the headboard with her.

She took another segment of the orange before asking, "My father is still a suspect in my abduction?"

"He is."

"Then, when you talk to him, ask him where

my violin is, please." She shook her head and picked up a slice of cheese, placing it on top of the buttered baguette he'd put on her tray.

Harbinger lifted his eyebrows but finished sipping his wine before asking, "What do you mean?"

"I was playing it when I was taken in Corsica. I went out into the field behind the houses, far enough I wouldn't be heard. That was where I was attacked. I remember it falling from my hands as the needle went into my neck. When I woke up in that cell, it wasn't with me."

"Your Stradivarius?"

"Yes." She nodded. "I shouldn't be worried about it when your friend Smith is hurt, and my father is ... but it's my ..." She shrugged.

"That violin is more than an instrument. It's the way you express yourself. It's an extension of who you are."

She smiled at him. "You understand. You always have."

Harbinger rolled his head to look at her. "The first time I watched you play, I remember thinking you and I had the same concentration of effort when working. You were focused on being the best you could possibly be. But I changed my mind about that assumption after watching you again. Your concentration isn't on being the best; it's on making your violin's music become something more than what's written on the page. You try to touch the heavens with your music, and when you do, you take the rest of us on a journey we'd never be able to go on alone."

Ysabel's big brown eyes misted. She swallowed hard before saying, "You say the most wonderful things to me." She put the cheese and bread back down on the plate.

"I'll stop unless you keep eating." He motioned to the food.

She laughed quietly. "I'll eat."

"And I'll always tell you how beautiful you and your music are." He cocked his head when he heard Con's voice in his ear. "Cloned phone has an incoming text."

Harbinger held up his finger when Ysabel started to say something. He pointed to his ear and mouthed, *Sorry*.

She smiled and went back to eating.

"A picture of a woman holding up today's paper."

Harbinger tapped his earpiece three times. "Hold on. When you were in the cave today, did someone take a picture of you with a paper in your hands?"

Ysabel shook her head. "No. When he slapped the paper on my chest, I didn't catch it, and when he bent over to pick it up, that's when I crashed the rock on his head."

"It isn't Ysabel," Harbinger said.

"Well, then, it's an AI mock-up and a damn good one," Con replied.

"Send it to my cell phone." Harbinger got off the bed and went to the vanity where he'd placed his cell.

He stared at the picture that appeared. Ysabel came up behind him. "She looks like me, but she isn't bruised." Ysabel leaned closer. "Her hair is obscuring her face. Look, she's clean. Look at her fingernails. They probably put my face on someone else, but it isn't perfect. My cheekbones are higher, and my chin isn't as sharp, so they didn't take time to make it right. My father will be able to tell this isn't me."

"That picture *wasn't* manipulated," Jewell said. "Facial rec hits on both Ysabel Archambeau and Nadia Molchalin. Nadia's match is ninety-seven percent. Ysabel forty-three percent."

"Her sister," Con said.

"Which implicates her in the hostage-taking, not Ysabel's father." Jewell said what Harbinger was thinking.

"But her father knew she was missing. I still like him as the orchestrator of the entire thing." Con rebuffed Jewell's theory.

"We'll find out in the morning. Is there anything new on Smith?" Harbinger asked, stilling the running chatter.

"Nope. Waiting on word from our doc or Val. All we know is he was taken up to get pictures to see if that bullet fractured," Jewell informed him.

"All right. I'm going back to listening mode." He hit the earpiece three times and heard the beep, signaling he was clear to talk. "Nothing new on Smith."

"What did they say about that picture?" Ysabel had put on her clothes while he'd been listening to the computer techs.

"They're working on it, but they don't think it's been manipulated." He turned and extended his hand. "Do you want something else to eat?"

"No. Thank you. I'd like a glass of wine, and I want you to sit with me and hold me."

"That can be arranged." Harbinger poured her a small amount of wine, and they walked to the loveseat in the corner of the room. Harbinger turned on the gas to the fireplace and lit it before he sat down and cradled her into his side.

"If they didn't manipulate the photo, how did they find someone who looks so similar to me?" Ysabel took a sip and sighed heavily. "You know, there were times I didn't think I'd ever see you again. This, just being with you, is so much more than I believed would happen."

"What did you think would happen?" Harbinger didn't touch the photo question. He would have to reveal she had a sister sooner or later, but tonight wasn't the night. Tonight was about finding each other again ... and making sure Smith and Val were okay.

"That they would kill me. They weren't above hitting me and shoving me around. I knew they were keeping me alive for a reason. I just didn't know what that reason could be."

Harbinger sighed and kissed the top of her head. "They will pay. Whoever it was that did this to you."

She took a small sip of the wine. "You mean my father?"

Harbinger was silent for a moment, trying to

phrase his words carefully. "Yes, or perhaps others."

"Heath?"

He looked down at her. "Yes?" His phone vibrated in his pocket.

Ysabel smiled and nodded to the phone. "Answer it. It's okay."

Pulling the phone from his pocket, he saw Val's name and answered it. "How is he?"

"He'll be fine. They're removing the fragment of the bullet and another piece that went much deeper. The Guardian doctor is doing that, and they'll hold him at least overnight, which means I'll be here, too."

"Do you need anything?"

"Everything I need is getting ready to go into the operating theater, but he'll be okay, and so will I. I'll call you in the morning."

"That works but call me if you need me."

"I won't," Val snapped back. "Sorry, I mean, he'll be fine."

"You have every right to worry. Do you need me or Con to come to the hospital?"

"No, God, no. I'm just going to sit and wait. Having anyone here would make me be social and talk and shit. I'm not in the mood."

"Then call if something unexpected happens."

"Not going to happen and stop saying it, asshole," Val reprimanded him.

"Sorry. Whatever it takes." He let her know he was there for her.

"As long as it takes." Val dropped the call.

"Is he okay?" Ysabel asked.

"He will be. Val won't be back tonight." He put the phone on the small table beside the loveseat. "What were you going to ask me?"

Ysabel looked down at her glass. "That when we knew Smith was okay, would you make love to me."

Harbinger took the glass from her hand and set it on the table. He framed her face with his hands. "I want nothing more than to make love to you all night long. You've been through so much. I don't want to pressure you."

Ysabel leaned into him. "I need you, Heath. I need to feel your love. I need to know this isn't a dream, that you're here, and I didn't lose you when I said those horrible words."

CHAPTER 13

*E*ntangled in a raging sea of emotions, Ysabel's heart ached with need. The desire, raw and soul-deep, was more than longing. The feeling had become a visceral burning for Heath's embrace. Her quietly whispered words were a base and desperate appeal for him to take her and banish the shadows of doubt her words and actions had caused.

True, they'd spoken. Heath's guttural admission of what her rejection cost him squeezed her heart like an iron fist. But words weren't enough to fully bridge them to the couple they once were. She sought absolution in his touch and closeness. Craving the loss of self in the rhythm of their bodies and once again witnessing his unguarded shattering when he climaxed to see the raw truth in his eyes at that moment. To feel the reassuring weight of him against her and the gentle heave of his chest as he caught his breath was a longing she couldn't ignore.

The treasures of these moments of their love—the passion, heat, and physical touch—created sweeter music than she could ever dream of playing. She longed for the pure notes of unguarded truth to reverberate through her soul and echo in the very essence of her heart again.

Heath stood and extended his hand to her. He led her over to the bed and turned, facing her. He pulled her into a kiss that was anything but gentle. Ysabel let go of the fear of losing him and molded her body against his.

She pulled at his shirt, demanding the feel of his skin. He broke the kiss and ripped his shirt off before gently tugging hers off, too. His hands covered her breasts, and his lips found hers. God, she'd missed that. Heath controlled her body with the gentlest of touches. Anything he wanted from her, she'd immediately surrender. Yet he never asked for more than she could give. He finished undressing them while they continued to kiss and explore newly exposed skin. The ripple of his back muscles under her hands reminded her of the strength he possessed. He held her as he lowered her to the bed. Crawling over her, his eyes scanned her body. He lowered and nipped at her shoulder. "Mine," he growled.

"Yes," she gasped as he slid his tongue over the sting of his bite. His hands and mouth were ravenous. Heath moved rapidly as if he couldn't get enough of her taste. His kisses stole her breath, and his touch made her pant with a growing need. When he dipped between her legs, she slammed her hands down on the bed and fisted the blankets. His tongue and fingers worked her sensitive skin until she tightened like a bow. He sucked her clit into his mouth, and she detonated, coating him in the proof of her love. She grabbed two handfuls of his hair and pulled him away from her, overstimulated yet still in need of him inside her. She wrapped her legs around his waist and pulled him down for a kiss.

He entered her as their tongues danced to the beautiful music that once again swirled in perfect harmony around them. She couldn't imagine a sweeter, more encompassing sensation than his body inside of her. It wasn't the act of sex. She stared into those beautiful hazel eyes. No, it wasn't sex; it was a testament to something time, words, or acts could never destroy. As she tightened again, Heath held her gaze. Her eyes widened, and he stared down at her. "You are mine. Now and always." His hips sped up, and he hilted harder inside her. "I'll never let you go again. You're mine. I love you." Each word was stressed by the feel of his shaft delving deeper and harder.

Ysabel arched under him and burst into nothing but frissons of pleasure. She forced her eyes open and watched as Heath followed her into oblivion. As their eyes met, she knew they would be okay. He collapsed on top of her, a weight she loved to hold. As she wrapped her arms around his magnificent body, she tried to memorize the aura and sensations surrounding her. She'd never take them for granted again.

Heath moved off her and pulled her with him. His hand stroked her hair, and she snuggled against his shoulder. The scent of him and their lovemaking filled her senses. "I love you," she whispered against his skin as he held her.

He kissed the top of her head and wrapped his other hand around her. "Never again."

She nodded. Never again would they let words or the world tear them apart. Heath had told her that her music took people places they couldn't go. Yet it was his love that carried her. Ysabel closed her eyes and floated on the orchestra of music in her heart.

* * *

HARBINGER WOKE to the familiar weight of Ysabel's leg and arm draped over him. Her hair, as usual, sprayed across his chest, and her head was cradled on his shoulder. He'd almost convinced himself that simple pleasure would never happen again. *Almost.*

His earpiece had been silent all night. The techies had probably switched to another channel. Val hadn't called, so he assumed all went well with the surgery. The question now was what to do with Ysabel. He had to interrogate her father. He'd never bring Pierre to Val's place, and leaving Ysabel alone was out of the question. He stared at Val's closet as he thought. A smile flicked across his face. Of course. He'd use Val's clothes and makeup to shroud Ysabel's identity. He could take her into the building without anyone knowing it was her.

Ysabel stretched and snuggled closer to him. "Morning," she mumbled.

"Good morning." He lifted his arm, bringing her closer to him and kissing her hair. "Did you sleep well?"

"Mmm…" She was a slow starter in the morning. Waking up wasn't her strong suit. Harbinger smiled at the warm memories of them waking up together. They had a second chance, and he'd never let her slip through his fingers again. The shock of her words and Pierre's concerted effort to keep him away, then that voicemail where she called him pathetic … Never again. She sighed contently. He would wait and be quiet and let her fall back to sleep, but her hand snaked under the sheets and found his cock. His morning wood hardened with interest.

"Definitely a *good* morning," he amended his previous statement.

She chuckled and slid under the sheets. "What?" Harbinger jumped a bit. The move was one she'd never done before. Oh, yeah, she'd given him head, but never like that.

"Do I have to explain?" She licked a stripe up his shaft.

His hips bucked, and he fell back on the pillows. "No. No explanation required." His hand wound around the long strands of thick black hair and held her. Not to guide her but to ground himself in the moment.

The feel of her velvet-soft, wet, hot mouth over the top of his cock made his eyes roll backward in his head. The slide and velvet swipe of her tongue were things wet dreams were made of. Ysabel wasn't a virgin when they met, but she wasn't very experienced either. But this … this was masterful. Her hand circled the bottom of his shaft and pumped up as she went down. The swirl of her tongue on the way back up made his thighs quake with the effort not to thrust into her mouth. The perfection of hot, wet suction brought him to the edge far too quickly. He tried to get her to stop, but she hummed something around his cock, causing his back to arch, and he exploded. She swallowed everything he gave her, and when the sensation was too much, he convulsed with a spine-cracking shiver. Harbinger pulled her off him, lifting her up the bed before wrapping his arms around her. "God, woman, what was that for?"

"You," she whispered and sighed against his chest. "No matter what happens from here on out, I'm yours, and you're mine."

While stroking her hair, he closed his eyes. "I still have your engagement ring."

Her head popped up, and she blinked rapidly. "You do?"

He nodded. "In my safe at the apartment. When we go there, I'll put it back on your finger where it belongs."

"You still want to marry me?" The question surprised him.

"I've never stopped wanting that." He rolled them so she was under him. "I've never stopped wanting you." He lowered for a kiss. The world and all its problems could wait another hour … or two.

CHAPTER 14

"How did you learn how to do this?" Ysabel turned this way and that, looking at herself in the mirror.

"In another life, I studied theater arts," Harbinger said as he took one of Val's long red wigs off one of the many mannequin heads holding an array of wigs in every color imaginable.

Ysabel looked up at him. "How did you get into security, then?"

He flipped the wig over and helped her put it on. "I found out I had an affinity for my particular branch of security. Not many do."

"What branch is that?" she asked as she smoothed the red waves. "I can't believe I'm under all this."

"You're much more beautiful as you, but this will do for today." Harbinger avoided the question about his branch of security.

"You didn't answer my question."

Or maybe not. "I'm a troubleshooter. I go in when all other measures have failed, and I work to rectify the problem."

"Digital?" she asked as she stepped into Val's white leather pants.

"No. Physical." He handed her a white silk shirt and a pair of leopard print boots.

"So, like bars on a cell and things like that?" she asked as she dressed.

"Something like that, but my nondisclosure agreement doesn't let me discuss anything about the particulars." And taking out the most vile and reprehensible monsters who walked the earth were particulars she didn't need to hear.

"How do I look?" She stood four inches taller than normal in the boots, and the hair and makeup changed her appearance enough that identifying her would be almost impossible. "Like a redhead." He walked up and kissed her. "I prefer you without makeup." He kissed her again. "And clothes."

She laughed and swatted at him with her hand. "Didn't I satisfy you this morning?"

"I'll never have enough of you." He grabbed her and lowered her into a back-bending dip. She grabbed his shoulders and held on. "I've got you. Let go and trust me." He watched as she relaxed in his arms. Only then did he kiss her until they were both breathless. Then he stood them up and stared at her. "Are you ready?"

She nodded. "With you by my side, I'm ready for anything." They walked to the front room together. "Did Val say when Smith would be released from the hospital?"

"She said if he wasn't released by the doctor today, Smith would check himself out against medical advice. I'm not sure Val will allow that, though. They want to make sure he doesn't develop an infection. There wasn't too much damage done by the bullet, and they were able to repair the damage to the chest muscle." Val said the doctor had to do some fancy stitching, but the muscle would heal.

Harbinger put on his suit jacket and pulled his shirt sleeves down. He glanced around the apartment. Val had her keys, and he'd lock the door on the way out. "Remember, when your father is at my apartment, he can't see you or know you're there. I won't be able to get the truth from him if he knows."

Ysabel sighed, "I hope, here"—she placed her hand on her heart—"that what you believe is wrong."

Harbinger nodded. "I know you do, and for your sake, I hope I'm wrong, too." But he wasn't. The man was involved in a web of crimes and lies. He knew it the same way he knew Ysabel was his. Gut instinct. He'd learned to trust those feelings. They never led him astray.

They left the apartment and walked from the building to the waiting car. They were less than two miles from his apartment. As they pulled up to the building, he saw a new person in position, watching the front door of his building. "Ready?"

"Yes." She nodded and whispered, "Get out, laugh, and look straight at the guy and then wink at him." Ysabel spoke even quieter to him even though the privacy shield was up on the limo. "Are you sure that won't alert him?"

Harbinger smiled at her. "I'm positive. If you aren't afraid of him seeing you, his natural instinct will be to discount you as a person he's interested in. It's human nature. He's looking for someone else, not a redhead."

She touched her wig. "I'm ready."

Harbinger opened the door and exited, extending his hand back for her. Ysabel stepped out gracefully and gave a full throaty laugh. It caught the man's attention, and he stood away from the building to get a good look at her. Harbinger moved out of the man's line of sight, and Ysabel turned to look at the posted sentry. She smiled widely and then winked at the posted outlook. The man blinked and turned away. Harbinger hid a smile as he wrapped Ysabel's hand in the crook of his elbow and escorted her into the building.

They didn't speak until he unlocked it and walked into his apartment. "That was some show," Con said from the hallway door.

Ysabel squeaked and jumped at his voice.

"Oh, crap, was I supposed to stay hidden?" Con's eyes widened as he ping-ponged his stare from Harbinger to Ysabel.

"No. Con, this is Ysabel. Ysabel, this is Con. He's one of our techies and is helping us figure out who's involved in your kidnapping."

Ysabel smiled shyly at him. "Thank you."

"My pleasure," Con said with a little dip that maybe was supposed to be a bow or something.

"I've got the comms set up whenever you're ready to place that call, and I have the equipment I need for the other project."

Spike yowled and ran toward Ysabel. She dropped to her knees, and the cat literally jumped into her arms. "Spike. I missed you, too."

Harbinger smiled at the gyrations the cat was going through. He'd felt the same way when he'd first heard Ysabel's voice in that cavern. Nothing would keep him from her arms. He glanced at Con. "Give me a few minutes," Harbinger said before guiding Ysabel through to their bedroom.

She walked over to the bed and sat down, still stroking the cat. "It's so good to be home." She looked up at him. He walked over and lifted her chin with his finger. "I have many apartments and houses throughout the world. Home is wherever you are."

"You promised me something when we got here." Ysabel bit her lip as she tended to do when anxious. He bent down and kissed her before going to the safe in the small closet. Keying in the combination, he opened the door to reveal the black velvet box sitting alone in the safe. He lifted the box and opened the lid. Emeralds surrounded the square-cut diamond. He'd commissioned the ring and had it made just for her.

He walked back to her and dropped in front of her onto one knee. Taking the ring out, he waited for her to remove the ring her mother had given her. He slid it into place and lifted her hand, kissing it. "You took this off once. I won't survive if you take it off again."

Ysabel's eyes flooded with tears, and she once again dropped down with him. "There's nothing in this world that will tear me away from you again. I am yours. I always will be."

"And I am yours. Believe in me, Ysabel. Believe in us. No one comes between us."

"No one. I swear." She nodded. "I love you, Heath. When I thought I lost you, all I wanted was to tell you that. I love you."

"And you are my life. My life, Ysabel. Your love is the blood that keeps my heart beating. You are my reason." He dropped for a kiss, trying to convey the emotions his words couldn't.

"Ah … H? Did you call Pierre already?" Con called from somewhere in the hall.

Harbinger snapped his head up and looked in the direction of the hall. "No, why?" he called back.

"He's outside the building and coming in."

Harbinger stood up. "Your father is here. Please, stay here. Don't come out. I'll come back for you when we're done." He helped her to her feet.

Ysabel nodded, cradling her hand with the engagement ring. "I'll take off this makeup and wait for you."

Harbinger picked up her mother's ring and headed to the door. "Heath?"

He stopped and looked back at her. "He's still my father, even if he's done what you say. I ..." She sighed and looked up at him.

"You love him."

She dipped her head. "I hope it wasn't him."

"I know. Wait here." Harbinger stepped out into the hall and shut the door behind him. He tossed the ring to Con, who was in the hall. A pounding on the door sent Con back to the communications room. Harbinger hit his earpiece three times. "Ready?"

"Yep." Con's voice was in his ear. Harbinger strode to the door and opened it just as Pierre tried to land another round of pounding. The man fell into the apartment. Harbinger caught his arm, steadying him. Once again, it looked as if Pierre had lived through hell, unlike his appearance at the business when Harbinger had gone in as someone else.

"She's missing." Pierre ran his hands through his hair.

Harbinger glared at the man and crossed his arms. "We've established that."

"No, you don't understand."

Harbinger unbuttoned his suit and sat down. "Then explain it to me."

"I found out where she was being held in the catacombs. She was taken from Corsica and brought here. Held in the catacombs. I sent in some of my men who work security for me at my building with a map indicating her location in the catacombs. When they finally found where she was being held, they didn't find her; they found a man. The man in the cell was a raging bull of a man who attacked them. They killed him, and not knowing what else to do, they left to go back to the surface and contact me. Only whoever had moved Ysabel out of the cell was coming back, and my men opened fire. Two of my men were hit badly, and a third didn't make it. But they were able to get out and bring the dead and injured with them." Pierre sat down and covered his mouth with his hand.

"Holy shit. Smith took down three," Con whispered.

Harbinger leaned forward and stared at Pierre. "How did you find her location?"

"The catacombs? From the picture they sent of her," Pierre said dismissively.

"No, you said you sent them in with a map, meaning you *knew* where she was." Harbinger stood and slid his hand into his pocket. "I'm through with the lies, Pierre. Come clean about what the hell is going on, or I'm walking."

"Then you don't love her!" Pierre yelled at him.

"Believe what you will. Either you stop telling lies, or we're finished here. I asked for the list, and I asked for proof of life, but you have neither. How do I know you're not behind all of this?"

"I have proof of life!" Pierre pulled out the cloned phone and waved the picture at him. "It had to have been taken before my men got there."

Harbinger extended his hand for the phone, but Pierre slid it back into his pocket.

"Asshat doesn't want him to see it. He put it back in his pocket." Con's narration was obviously for others who were listening and watching on his security system.

"I want to see the photo," Harbinger demanded.

"Why? She isn't there anymore!" Pierre rasped and sat down in the chair. "She isn't there." A tear slid down his cheek.

"How do you know?" Harbinger demanded.

Pierre took the phone out of his pocket and tossed it to Harbinger. "That isn't Ysabel."

"Who has her?" Harbinger asked quietly.

Pierre shook his head. The look of guilt dripped from every pour in the man's body.

"Who are you working with? Who crossed you?" Harbinger screamed and grabbed Pierre by the tie. "For once in your fucking life, tell the truth."

"She told me she wouldn't hurt Ysabel."

He shook the older man. "Who?"

"Nadia."

After shoving the man backward into the chair, Harbinger lowered and whispered, "You have one chance to explain from the beginning. If you leave anything out, I swear I will strip your skin off your body piece by piece until you die."

Genuine fear seized the older man. That was an emotion with which Harbinger had an intimate relationship. "You *are* with the government."

Harbinger shook his head and, in the deadliest way, spoke in an utterly calm voice, almost too quiet to be heard. "No government can control what I am or what I do. Leave anything out, and no one will find any piece of what remains of you. *That* I can guarantee." Harbinger then repeated the threat in flawless French, Russian, and Spanish. In English, he hissed, "No, I do not work for the government, which is why you should be afraid. Talk now and leave nothing out. I will know."

Pierre swallowed hard. "Abrasha wants me to open four key fobs. The money belonged to people who failed him, and he had them eliminated."

"Where is the list?"

"There is no list for Abrasha." The man looked down. "I made a deal with the devil or, in this case, the devil's daughter."

"Meaning?"

"Nadia Molchalin approached me after her father demanded I open the fobs."

He'd circle back to Nadia in a minute. "How can Molchalin demand such a thing from you?"

"We've had dealings in the past. If I don't do as he says, he'll ensure my prior activities are exposed."

"Criminal." He wasn't surprised. "You haven't escaped your past, have you?" The man shook his head, and Harbinger continued, "How many times have you worked with Molchalin?"

"Too many to count. His projects are lucrative." Pierre closed his eyes momentarily. "I was forced the first time. After that …" The man's eyes misted, and he shrugged.

Pierre was acting again. The fucker wouldn't learn, would he? Harbinger changed his tactic. "Who's Nadia Molchalin?"

"His daughter by Léonie."

"Ysabel's sister," Harbinger said.

"Yes. Five years younger," the older man agreed.

"Why did you send Ysabel to Corsica?"

"I'm owed favors." The man shrugged. "I didn't know if Léonie's rambling letter was true. If she'd stolen information from Abrasha, he would naturally come after me and anyone important to me. It's *his* way. Not only the person responsible pays, but his entire family. I'm all Lèonie had outside that relationship. If he thought I was complicit, he would order my family and anyone important to my family killed. Her, you."

"You didn't give a flying fuck about me. You saw it as a way of getting me out of her life."

"What does it matter now? She's probably

dead," Pierre shot back. Only there were no tears now. Just anger.

A thought struck Harbinger, and he went with it. "Molchalin still doesn't know Ysabel is his daughter?"

"I don't think he does, but he might."

"How did he not know about her before if you worked with him?"

"He knew I had a daughter. I have no pictures, social media, any electronic trail to her."

"He's right about that," Jewell said, momentarily drawing his attention from Pierre. "She was in boarding school, then in the States studying at Juilliard. She has no social media."

Pierre continued, "Lately, I'm not often of value to him. I've never dealt with him in person. By phone or messenger only."

"But Ysabel would be important to Abrasha. She's a bargaining chip you've had stashed away, isn't she?"

Pierre just stared at him. The shock on his face was about being found out rather than the idea he'd raised Ysabel just to have security against a murderous bastard. There was no defense the asshole could give.

"That fits Archambeau's psych profile. Oh, hey

in case you want to see it, that came in last night," Con told him.

"Get more information on the other daughter," Fury demanded.

Harbinger cracked his neck, wanting everyone to shut up but not being able to say it. "What was Nadia's deal?"

"We were to split twenty billion in crypto. She'll provide the fobs." Pierre shrugged as if it were no big deal.

"How did she find out about Ysabel?"

Again, Pierre shrugged as if the information were inconsequential. "I don't know. I would guess Léonie, but I don't know."

"If Nadia knows Ysabel is her sister it would stand to reason Molchalin knows about her, too." Harbinger swore softly.

"No. After she was taken, Nadia said she would tell her father about Ysabel if I didn't crack the codes and surrender all the money."

"How did she find where Ysabel was hiding?"

"I don't know!" Pierre whined. The miserable face he made was for impact only. The act was easy to see through now. "Those who knew where she was are my closest allies."

"Then you have a snake in your midst." More

than one, it would seem. "Why did Nadia take her?"

"As I said, she decided she didn't want to split the money. She wants it all. She said she would return Ysabel after I deposited the money in the accounts she'll give me."

"She wanted you to deposit her father's money in her account, too?"

"No. She's not stupid. *No one* fucks with Abrasha. You wind up dead. I don't know where Ysabel is. There are almost three hundred kilometers of tunnels under this city. She hates the dark. You have to help me find her." Pierre rubbed his arms as if he were cold.

Harbinger chuffed a disbelieving huff of air. Ysabel and he had spent hours in the dark admiring the stars and talking. She wasn't afraid of the dark, or at least she hadn't been.

"Who's the woman in the photo?" Harbinger nodded to the phone.

"I don't know, but I would assume it's Nadia because she looks similar to Ysabel. I've only dealt with her on the phone and through messenger."

"How did she get you to agree to work with her if you didn't know her?"

"She had a very interesting calling card." Pierre

sighed. "The arm that was sent to me was from her."

"Your private detective?"

"Yes, after she contacted me, I wanted to ensure she was who she said she was. I hired this man to confirm it. I've been working on gathering the equipment, and people needed to complete the crypto exchange for Abrasha for seven months. The computer requirements to break through such passwords take much red tape and government approval. Ysabel was safe in Corsica when Nadia showed up a month before you came back and made me an offer I couldn't refuse."

Con barked out a laugh. "*Vito's line! The Godfather!*" Then, hastily added, "Sorry. Sorry."

Pierre kept talking. "I gave the detective the telephone number from which she'd called me. Four days later, I received his arm via messenger. Then Nadia sent that picture of Ysabel. My favors, it seemed, had run out with the family."

"We still need the list of whose crypto he's stealing." That was Archangel.

"Did Nadia provide you a list of whose crypto she was stealing?"

"I know those names. The fobs from Abrasha will arrive via armed messenger after I tell him I'm ready. The other twenty billion are to be stolen by my operators via a program Nadia will provide that night. She claims it can get into any system. She called it a nutcracker." Pierre shook his head. "I don't know how she'll get to the information. Crypto is held in the securest of digital vaults."

Harbinger walked over to a table by the wall, opened the drawer, and withdrew a pen and pad of paper. "Write the names down, and don't forget any."

"How will this help you find Ysabel?" Pierre stared at the paper when Harbinger dropped the pad in front of him.

"I'll let you know when you've given me the names." He watched as Pierre wrote in neat block letters a list of seven names. He handed the pad to Harbinger.

"He's got the list," Con said, once again narrating the action in the living room as if the others couldn't see what was going on through his apartment's security cameras.

"Tell him she's safe," Archangel commanded.

Harbinger complied with his directive. "Ysabel is safe."

Pierre stood up and reached for him. Harbinger

slapped the man's hands away in an instinctive move. Pierre jerked back. "Are you sure?"

"I'm positive."

"What can I do to repay you?" The weight of the world seemed to melt from Pierre's shoulders. But again, the act was easy to spot.

"She wants her violin."

"What?" Her father seemed to stagger momentarily.

"She wants her violin," Harbinger repeated.

Pierre frowned. "She has it." That was probably the most honest statement the man had said since he'd walked through the door.

"No, I assure you, she doesn't. I suggest you check with your friend Nadia."

"That woman is no friend of mine," Pierre spat out.

Harbinger lifted an eyebrow. "She's your business partner."

"Were you going to tell me Ysabel was safe?"

"Were you going to tell me the truth?" Harbinger countered.

Pierre sneered, which meant he'd probably bent the truth to make it fit his purposes. Whatever, Guardian would validate everything he'd said.

Pierre shoved his hands in the pockets of his slacks before asking, "Where is she?"

Harbinger shook his head. "No."

Pierre reeled back. "What do you mean no? She's my daughter. I have every right to know where she is."

"She's an adult, and in this situation, you've divested yourself of any rights. Ysabel is safe, and you are not," Harbinger clarified. "You have crypto to steal and two deadly Russians waiting for you to do so. *You* are not safe."

"I can protect her." Pierre lifted to his full five foot seven inches and drew back his shoulders.

Harbinger rolled his eyes. A puffer fish trying to make himself bigger, but he would never to be an important person. He was a criminal with the veneer of respectability. Just like the fuckers Harbinger took out for Guardian. A sneer lifted the corner of his lip as he spoke. "Obviously not. The people you hire are amateurs. The people you trust have betrayed you, and the people you do business with are deadly vipers. You've been bitten, Pierre. You just don't realize the venom is running through your veins, and you're already dead."

"Yet I've been smart enough to amass a fortune.

Don't think for a moment Ysabel will inherit a penny of my money. That's the only reason you attend to her. She's no beauty. She has no worth to anyone but me."

"Right, who will he leave it to, his mistress?" Jewell chuffed. "She's married with two kids. She could use it."

Harbinger gave Pierre a deadly smile. "I would love her even if she were penniless. Her beauty is unmatched because of the love and passion that live in her heart and soul and radiate out in the purest form. You're too blinded by greed to see that. Leave your money to your mistress—the one with two children and a husband."

Pierre's eyes grew wide with shock. Harbinger continued, knowing he had the man on the ropes, and suddenly realized what the asshole in front of him was. He was a classic psychopath. Why hadn't he seen it sooner? Harbinger cocked his head and said, "Ysabel doesn't need your money. What she needed was your love. But I'm not sure you have any to give." Which struck a chord deep inside him. The truth resonated with a crystal-clear toll. Pierre had been worried about Ysabel, but *not* how a father should be … "You didn't want to be under Abrasha and later Nadia's thumb. Ysabel was your get-out-of-jail-free card. *That's* why you hid her. Not for her safety. You didn't want us together because I could take her away from you. You used Léonie's death and Abrasha approaching you for this mission as a reason to split us up. A reason to force her into exile ... to keep your bargaining chip safe. You never wanted her, but you used her as window dressing to put a civil veneer on your criminal activities and as a trump card to play if needed."

"Damn. That's probably true based on his profile," Con said in his ear.

Jewell made a sound of agreement.

Pierre snarled, "You don't know me."

"Oh, yes, we do," Jewell said.

"Do not tell him we're working on the crypto theft," Archangel directed.

"Oh, but I do know you, Pierre. I also know you've written your own destiny." Harbinger picked up the list and tore off the top page, holding it in his hand.

"What are you going to do with the list?"

"Nothing, right now," Harbinger said as he pocketed the paper. "This is my insurance policy. I can send it and our conversation today to the police if you do something stupid. You don't think

I was inept enough *not* to record you, do you? This note is in your handwriting. Your words admitted your crimes. It would seem unusual, don't you think, that you had a list of the people the money will be stolen from before it happens? You're going to walk out that door and never come back. If Ysabel wants to talk with you, she can reach out when your little crypto caper is over … if you're still alive. In the meantime, as a gesture of goodwill, you'll find and return her violin. Let your daughter think you give a shit about her."

Pierre stared at him for a long moment before turning and walking out the door. The click of the latch echoed through the living room. Harbinger followed him and locked the deadbolt. The son of a bitch. How did he tell Ysabel her father was a psychopath?

"Ah, dude. Check the hallway." Con's voice carried to him through the earpiece.

Harbinger turned and walked to the wall. On the other side, Ysabel sat on the floor at the end of the hallway. Spike was curled up on her lap. Wiping at tears, she glanced up at him. "That was hard to hear." She tried to laugh.

Harbinger tapped his earpiece into listen mode as he sat down beside her. "I'm sorry you heard it."

"I'm not." She sniffed and leaned into his shoulder. "I wouldn't have believed it in my heart if I hadn't." She stroked the cat as tears dripped onto her hand. "He's in trouble."

"He is." Harbinger could only agree with her.

"Are you going to help him?" She glanced up at him quickly.

Did he want to? No. Would Guardian save the man from himself? Probably. Especially because her father had information about crimes committed by Abrasha. "Right now, I don't know what my company will do regarding your father. That's above my pay grade. What I do know is your safety is my primary concern."

She sighed, and he wrapped his arm around her shoulders. He half-listened as Con explained what was happening to the others who didn't have this video feed. The hallway and the bedrooms were not covered by the camera. His private areas were not open for anyone's viewing. "How much did you hear?"

She shrugged. "I came out about the time you asked him why he sent me to Corsica. I took off my makeup and changed. Then I wanted to hear. I know I should've stayed in the bedroom, but … He's not a good man, is he?"

"I don't think so, no," Harbinger admitted.

Ysabel was silent for a long time. Then she asked, "Are they going to kill him?" She sniffed and moved closer to him when Spike decided he wanted to leave.

Harbinger dropped his chin to the top of her head. "He's survived this long. That proves he's not as limited as I implied to him. I don't know the people he's aligned with, but my company does. They're criminals and have a violent background." And that was putting it mildly.

He felt her head nod under his chin. She asked, "Would you hate it if we didn't live in Paris? Or, for that matter, France?"

"Not at all. We can live anywhere." He'd be happy to be rid of the memories of the last eight months and live on with fresh memories and happier times.

"I'd like to go back to America. I had several job offers from the philharmonics and orchestras on the East Coast over the years."

"Then America it is."

"When?"

"As soon as I can arrange it with my bosses." They could get the hell out of dodge and leave that mess to someone else. "I like living in Europe, but if you have opportunities in America, then we'll go back. My team is there, and we'll have their support."

"I could look for other jobs?" She held up her hand. "I don't want you to be upset by moving."

"Upset?" Harbinger smiled. "Never. I'm an American, and I love my country. Moving home will not be a hardship. I'll still have to travel for work, but where I am isn't important. It's where *we* are that matters. Nothing else." He kissed the top of her head and felt her relax. They rested like that for a moment.

Ysabel whispered, "Who's Nadia?"

"Your sister." He wouldn't lie to her.

She looked up at him—the makeup he'd used to conceal her identity was gone. Instead, the light scattering of freckles bridged her nose. She was so beautiful. How her father couldn't see her beauty and worth was impossible to comprehend.

"Sister?"

"Yes, five years younger."

"They kept her, but not me." Ysabel cocked her head and closed her eyes. She drew a deep breath in and let it out slowly. "That hurts, and yet I'm glad she gave me up. I don't think growing up with her would've been the best environment for me."

Harbinger nodded and stroked her arm where his hand rested. "If things had been different, we might not have met."

When she shivered, he tightened his hold on her. "I don't ever want to imagine a world where you're not here with me."

"Neither do I."

"H, the bosses want a word." Con's voice came through his device loud and clear.

"The bosses want to talk to me," he relayed.

"I'll make lunch," Ysabel said as he stood and helped her up from the floor. "Is Con staying here?"

"If she's fixing food, you can't kick me out."

Harbinger rolled his eyes and tapped his earpiece. Then he turned and looked at the almost microscopic camera at the top of the door. "Stop eavesdropping."

"But, dude, I'm famished."

Harbinger turned his back on the camera. "He's staying in the guest room, and yes, he's hungry."

Ysabel managed a smile. "I'll make extra then." She toed up and kissed him. "I love you."

CHAPTER 15

Harbinger squeezed Ysabel's hand before releasing it at the juncture of the hallway, where he watched her until she entered the kitchen. He glowered at the camera as he headed into the second bedroom, shutting and locking the door behind him. Ysabel didn't need to know about the comm room.

Con turned as he walked in. "Sorry, man. Don't unalive me. But I missed breakfast."

Harbinger stopped. "Unalive you? What's that supposed to mean?" Con was a smart techie, but he was also a bit annoying.

"That's online speak for don't kill him," Jewell said from the monitor where the others were called up.

"I wouldn't mind if you unalived him," Joseph said quite calmly.

"Joseph." Archangel sighed.

"Just saying." Joseph spread out his hands in front of him. "Wouldn't bother me."

"I'm not killing anyone right now, but I really want to strangle Ysabel's father." Harbinger sat down in the chair in front of the camera. "I don't trust a thing he said. For the most part, my gut was telling me he was acting. I'm sure he's a psychopath, and he's damn good at cloaking it. I wasn't looking for it before, but I can tell you everything I saw and heard is telling me Pierre doesn't give a shit about Ysabel. He *was* pissed the violin was missing."

"Because the one she uses cost him over one point five million euros," Jewell said. "There was a big article in a Parisian magazine about him buying it. Nothing about him giving it to his daughter or, for that matter, that he *had* a daughter, just the fact that he now owned it. It isn't the rarest out there, but it's mid to high level. But that isn't what I keyed in on. The Nutcracker." Jewell stared at the camera, seeming to age in front of him. "If Nadia has that program, she'll be able to get the electronic version of the fobs. The nutcracker wasn't made to break the electronic keychain, just firewalls. That's why she'd need Pierre to break the passcode for crypto."

"That program all flows back to Dean Kowalski." Jacob King tossed his pen down on the desk in front of him and leaned back. "The Kowalskis are a gift that keeps on giving, aren't they?"

Harbinger leaned forward. "Kowalski, as in the Guardian traitor?"

Archangel nodded. "The perp here is actually his cousin, but yeah, same family."

"We have the list of names. We can try to find where the crypto is being held …" Con rubbed his forehead. "But what do we do, say, hey, you're being targeted by the Russian mob, which isn't true, just the rogue daughter of a Russian oligarch who would kill you and your family rather than look at you?"

"He really does talk just to hear the noise." Joseph sighed.

Archangel leaned on his elbows. "We don't know for a fact she has a copy of the program or that she has people who know how to use it. Her intent to access the money isn't a crime."

"Actually, stealing it is, and it is actionable. So, when we take her down, we find out if she used the program. If she did, we can leverage that information in an interrogation to get the names of those who gave it to her and who currently have it," Jared King said from the bottom right-hand corner of the screen. Harbinger had only seen him a couple of times, and that was usually if the criminal he was tracking was involved in crimes in the United States. The man was in charge of Domestic Operations.

"She's not a US citizen. How are we going to interrogate her?" Con frowned at the screen. Joseph chuckled evilly, and Con's eyebrows shot up. "Oh. Never mind."

"With permission from the government of the country where she'll be arrested. Guardian has agreements in place." Archangel chuckled. "Nothing as nefarious as Fury would have you believe. So, where are we with a geographic location for the heist?"

"We're down to three buildings. One really doesn't fit the needs because it's small and doesn't have the power output or comm structure for a supercomputer connection, but it could depend on how many programmers Pierre hires."

"How many would you need?" Jacob King asked.

"Five," Con and Jewell said at the same time, laughing.

"So, concentrate on the other areas. Fury, send Jinx to both locations and find out what he can see."

"Done. Button, send me the locations." Fury leaned forward as he spoke.

"Rog-O," Jewell replied.

"I need to get Ysabel out of here," Harbinger said. She could wait for him in the States.

"I take it you want to remain to wrap this up?" Archangel asked.

"You couldn't get me out of this op if you held a gun to my head," Harbinger confirmed.

Archangel sighed and leaned forward. "All right. We need to get Smith and Val home. He's threatening to check himself out of the hospital, but our doctor is gravely concerned about an infection he's developed. They caught it quickly, but the doc wants to treat it at the hospital before he's air-evacuated home. Val will be with him, as will the Guardian doctor. We can take Ysabel out on the same aircraft. I don't feel comfortable using public transportation with the Corsican Mafia still watching your building. That's a card that hasn't been turned over, and we don't know its purpose. I won't take chances with one of ours."

Harbinger blinked and then smiled. "Thank you for that."

Archangel frowned. "Of course, the second you brought your intentions with Ysabel to Smoke, she became ours."

"Remind me to kick Smoke, will you?" Fury said.

"Why?" Harbinger asked. "He's my mentor, and I kept him advised."

Fury growled, "Because I happen to be your boss, not him. I should throttle the little shit."

"You're pretty murderous; you know that, right?" Con flipped the question to Fury.

"And yet you keep forgetting it," Fury snapped.

"And enough of that. Con, have you made any progress on the documents in the ring?" Archangel stopped the exchange.

"I'm waiting on a delivery. I have almost everything I need, but according to what I've read, the magnification needed to be able to read the plate is beyond anything I could get commercially. Jewell was able to order the lens I needed from an optical maker in Barcelona. I'll be able to take a photo of the documents and feed it into the computer to compile a digitized version. Depending on how much is on the plate, it could take a hot minute to complete."

"Have you removed it from the stone?" Jared King asked. "From what my forensics team told me, that could damage the plate if not done properly."

Con nodded. "I was able to order the solution my research on the dark web indicated was the best to loosen the plate from the resin. It will melt the resin but not hurt the laser etching."

"I confirmed the solution's adequacy with our contacts," Jewell added.

"H, are you good with keeping Ysabel at your residence, or do you need to use a safe house?"

"No. She's safe here." He wouldn't let a fucking thing happen to her; that was for sure.

"Then we have our tasks. I want everyone copied on the location where we expect Pierre to work. I want it covered and monitored for activity. Jacob, use one of your teams to provide that security, but they aren't to be seen."

"Not a problem," Jacob acknowledged.

"Let's get to work. Archangel out."

Con cleared the screen. He turned to Harbinger and, with the goofiest look on his face, asked, "Do you think lunch is ready?"

He rolled his eyes. "I'll go see."

CHAPTER 16

Ysabel stood staring out the kitchen window. What her father had said shattered her heart. There had always been a distance between them she didn't understand. The lack of participation in her life had always been explained away by business, wanting to keep her safe, or any other manner of excuse. Yet she'd always loved him with the adoration of a daughter for her father.

She chuffed a sad laugh and spoke to the universe. "You'd think after all you've been through this wouldn't matter."

"It matters because you feel betrayed," Heath said as he walked into the kitchen. She turned, leaned against the counter, and crossed her arms.

"I do," she admitted. He assumed a position mimicking hers, leaning against the counter across from her. "All of this has been surreal. I'm not sure how to process the hurt and anger."

"If you need help, I'm here, and we can set up appointments in the States so you can talk to a professional. There's no need to try to grapple with this alone."

"When do we leave?" She couldn't wait to put Paris behind her.

"Guardian is sending a plane for Val and Smith; you'll be on that. Smith has developed a seriously bad attitude. The doctor won't let him out of the hospital quite yet. But you'll be on the plane when they leave. I don't know exactly when."

Ysabel snapped her head up at that comment. "*I'll* be on the plane, not *we*?" She shot her finger from herself to him.

Heath nodded. "I'm staying here to wrap up things."

"With my father?"

"And others," Heath amended. "It's part of my job with Guardian."

"What exactly do you do for Guardian?" She held up a hand. "I think I have the right to know."

"I'm a troubleshooter. I take care of problems," he repeated his earlier statement. She shook her head.

"What do you do, Heath?"

Heath walked over to her side of the kitchen and turned to lean against the counter beside her. With a sigh, he told her, "What I do is not something I can discuss in any detail. I handle security breaches, and I eliminate situations that cause danger to innocent lives. That's *all* I can say. You'll have to trust that what I do is important and held in the strictest of confidence. I *cannot* talk about it."

"And Val and Smith do this, too?"

"Yes, but each of us has our own area of expertise."

"And yours is?"

"Classified, as is theirs." Heath shook his head. "If I could tell you, I would, but there's a line I can't cross, and I won't." He turned toward her. "Some things shouldn't ever be discussed. What I do for my company is one of them."

Ysabel stared at the man she loved. He was trying to tell her something … She blinked and then frowned. "Is what you do legal?"

Heath barked out a laugh and rubbed his neck.

"What I do has passed through so many layers of oversight. Each time we're sent out to take care of a situation, every 'I' has been dotted, and every 'T' has been crossed multiple times. Of that, I can assure you."

She looked down at the marble tile of the opulent apartment. "Is it dangerous?"

His finger touched her chin and lifted it up. She gazed into his eyes. "Sometimes, but I am a trained professional. I don't take risks. Especially since I met you." He held her gaze. "I know you want more definitive answers, but I can't give them to you." He dropped his hand. "I need to know if this is going to cause an issue between us."

Ysabel frowned. Her emotions were all over the place, but one thing she was sure of was that Heath's job was the least of her worries. She sighed and shook her head. "Of course not. Why would it? I can understand the requirements you work under. I'm so jumbled in the brain right now." The timer on the oven went off, and she reached over to turn it off. She turned around and bumped into Heath. "Whoa! Sorry."

"I'm not. You can be jumbled, confused, worried, hurt, or just plain mad, but none of those emotions should be centered around us. I am here for you, and I will always be as open as I can be about my job, but there will be limitations. I won't let anything put distance between us again." He lowered his mouth to hers, and she wrapped her arms around his neck. The kiss stopped the swirling thoughts. It stilled her emotional turmoil and halted the anxiety that had been wrapped around her.

"Hey, is lunch—"

Con's voice pulled them apart.

"Yeah, sorry. Should I go back to my room now?"

Heath twisted around. "I'm starting to understand the unalive comment now."

Ysabel frowned. "What are you talking about?"

Heath sighed and turned back to her. "He has a habit of interrupting things he shouldn't."

"It's one of my super skills, along with all things computer," Con added. "Whatever. Your cooking smells amazing."

Heath dropped his head to her shoulder. "Feed him before I tape him to the ceiling, please."

That image popped into her head, and Ysabel laughed. If someone had told her five minutes ago she'd laugh today or even tomorrow, she'd have thought they were crazy. But Heath was a balm for her soul and the one she loved more than life itself.

She hugged her man and said, "Go sit down. I'll bring you both food."

Con clapped his hands together and made straight for the table. Heath's coworker was amusing in a slightly annoying way. She pulled the quiche out of the oven along with a sheet pan of fries. She served the food and retrieved a light salad out of the fridge to accompany the lunch.

"Fries and quiche, I haven't had this in forever."

"Thank Heath's housekeeper; she stocks the freezer well, and I'm not a good chef."

"She's being modest." Heath winked at her. "She makes the best chili and cornbread."

"Chili?" Con stopped with a forkful of quiche halfway to his mouth. "I know that's not a thing over here." He frowned. "Or it wasn't the last time I was here."

"I studied at Juilliard in America and lived with a host family. They were from the south. Until then, I'd never cooked. They decided that needed to be remedied, and I learned their recipes."

"Well, this is good," Con said before he looked

over at Heath. "I have a delivery coming in tomorrow via Guardian."

Heath nodded and started to speak, but a beeping sound from Con's watch stopped him. Con glanced at his watch and then smiled. "Val is here and coming up."

Ysabel cocked her head. "How do you know?"

Con's eyes shot to her and then to Heath. "Ah ... she texted me?" He dropped his arm and scooped up another bite of food.

Of course, she wasn't thinking straight. Heath wiped his mouth and headed into the living room. She heard Val's voice and a low conversation before they entered the kitchen. Ysabel stood up. "Would you like some lunch?"

Val shook her head. "Thank you, no. I had cake salé at the hospital with Smith."

"How's the big guy?" Con asked, still eating.

"Pissed. He wants to get back to work. I told him we were heading home when the doctor releases him. That wasn't the right thing to say. Smith can be stubborn, and he wants to see the end of this situation. The Guardian doctor told him that if he had to knock him out with drugs to keep him in the hospital, he would."

Ysabel almost choked on her quiche. She

cleared her throat before asking, "Can they do that?"

Val laughed and shook her head. "No, but that's what it took for Smith to believe the doctor was serious. I needed to take a shower and get him some clothes. He is *so* over the hospital. I'm appeasing him by bringing him something other than the ill-fitting hospital johnnies."

"His injury is my fault." Ysabel sighed. "I don't know how to apologize."

Val held up her hand, silencing Heath, who had opened his mouth to interject. She leaned forward. "Because you don't need to apologize. Smith wasn't shot by you. You didn't stage your own kidnapping, and you had no idea there were armed people down there. There is absolutely nothing for you to apologize for. This isn't on you." She glanced over at Heath. "You should have told her that."

Heath's forehead furrowed. "I have, and you would've known that if you hadn't shoved your hand in my face."

Val leveled a look at him. "Did I offend your sense of propriety?"

Con laughed. "You guys are just like children."

"We've been coworkers forever." Val dismissed Con's observation. "Did he really tell you?"

"Hey!" Heath lifted his hands in the air. "Like I lie?"

"He's told me," Ysabel confirmed. "Still ..."

Val lifted her hand and waved off her concern. "Not your monkey, not your zoo."

Ysabel's eyes widened. "What does that mean?"

Con snorted. "You don't have to worry about it."

Val cocked her head and pointed to Ysabel. "How did you get her here? The assholes are still outside."

"A disguise. We borrowed some of your things," Heath replied.

"You're welcome to anything I have." She turned to Con. "I'm heading back to the hospital. Would you please do your thingy again for me? Flack wants you to call him. It's nothing urgent, but he's had experience with a project you're working on. Something about flats. I have no idea what that means, but I said I'd deliver the message because I was coming over anyway." Val got up from the table. "I have to get back before Smith decides he's over it and just leaves."

"I've got you. Just let me know when you're

nearing the hospital." Con got up from the table and took his lunch dishes to the sink. "I'll call Flack after that. I can use all the help he can give me on that project. Ysabel, thank you for lunch." Con followed Val out of the kitchen. "I'll lock up after her," Con said, stopping Heath from getting up.

"That was a whirlwind." Ysabel laughed.

"Always is with Val." Heath rose and took his plate and hers to the sink. "I think you should come with me." He held out his hand toward her.

"But the dishes." Ysabel turned toward the mess.

"They can wait. I need dessert."

"Dessert?" Ysabel lifted an eyebrow. She knew what type of sweet the man wanted.

He glanced back at her and winked. "I have a craving for lace."

HARBINGER WANTED to be inside the woman with an urgency he'd never felt. So much in their world was upside down. Her father was a bastard of the highest caliber, and he didn't doubt Pierre never once told the truth. Especially when Harbinger had questioned him.

He pulled her into the bedroom and shut the door, locking it behind him.

She tapped him on the chest, and he released her. She gasped for breath, but her hands kept moving across his chest. "Take that thing out of your ear and make sure he can't hear us."

It took Harbinger two seconds to comply with that wish. He tossed the earpiece onto the dresser after turning it off, and they fell onto the bed together. Ysabel laughed, and that musical lilt was the most beautiful sound in the world.

She pulled at the fabric of his shirt, and he lifted onto his knees over her, pulling it over his head. A button or two popped off in the process, but he didn't give a shit. Her hands were unbuckling his belt. He half growled, half groaned as her hand slid up and down his shaft when he reached down to take over for her.

He was off the bed and out of his clothes in no time. Then he leaned forward and crawled to her from the bottom of the bed. Stopping at her waist, he licked a strip of exposed skin. She folded in and grabbed his hair. They both knew what was coming next.

Harbinger unfastened her slacks and pulled them down, and she kicked them off before he settled down on his elbows. The mint green lace panties were ones that had been in her drawer when she was gone. He couldn't believe he was finally able to rip them off her. His tongue traced the small elastic band at the top and flicked over her hot skin. Gooseflesh rose when he gently blew across the wet trail his tongue had left. His fingers wrapped around the thin waistband at her hips. He lifted his head and smiled at her.

"Do it," she panted.

He snapped the elastic and dropped his head. The taste of her was beyond words. Sweet, warm, and essential as air. He spread her flesh and found her clit. She bucked up to meet his mouth. Harbinger belted her hips to the bed and worked her clit with his mouth as his fingers moved inside her. He loved the small sound she made, the way her hands searched for an anchor in the sheets and her legs trembled as he pushed her toward orgasm.

When she tightened under him, he sucked her clit into his mouth. The action shattered her. She tried to arch under his arm that held her down. Her soft moan pulsed in rhythm with her orgasm. He released her flesh when she crashed below him. He kissed his way up her body, gathered her into his arms, and entered her.

As her arms roped around him, she nuzzled into his neck. She kissed his throat, biting a bit here and there. The zing of that little bit of pain about undid him, and she knew it. His stroke broke when she sucked the skin on his chest into her mouth, marking him. Fuck. He put a bit of space between them, reached down, found her core, and ensured she was climbing that mountain with him.

They moved together, his body and hers in perfect harmony, until she crashed under him. It took two strokes for his orgasm to slam into him and explode his reality into a billion pieces. He dropped his head to her shoulder and shivered when her hand trailed up his spine to the base of his neck. "I love you," he whispered into her shoulder.

She chuckled. "I'll never tire of hearing that, but we do need to address this hatred you have for my undergarments."

He laughed and dropped to his side, pulling her with him. "On the contrary, I love that lace."

"Love to destroy it."

"True." He pulled her closer and draped his leg over hers.

"Everything will work out, right?" she asked after several moments.

"For us?" He looked down at her.

"Yes."

"They already have." He dropped down for a kiss. "We're going to be happy, married and together. Nothing will get in the way of that." He'd kill to make sure of it.

CHAPTER 17

"I don't know what to take. I thought we'd have more time before Smith was released." Ysabel looked from the closet to the suitcase on the bed.

"Evidently, Smith is not an easy patient and wants out of that hospital. Take whatever you're comfortable in and enough for a couple of weeks. I'm sure Val will take you shopping as soon as Smith goes back to work. Val loves shopping." He took out his matte black credit card and lifted it in two fingers. "I'm giving you this to use for anything you need while I'm gone. There's no limit on it, so have a good time with Val."

"No limit?" Ysabel smiled and reached for the card. Harbinger lifted it a bit, stalling her grasp.

"But you have to promise me you'll buy some lacy underwear."

She wrapped her arms around his neck. "But you ruin them."

"Because they take too long to take off." Harbinger lowered his head and kissed her. Sighing, she leaned into him, and he wrapped his arms around her and pulled her closer.

"Ah, dude … You have an incoming call from Pierre. This is the second call in the last two minutes." Con's yell down the hallway broke them apart.

Harbinger lifted his head and groaned. "I will be so glad when he's gone."

"Con is a sweetheart." Ysabel laughed and took the credit card, putting it in her handbag with her passport.

He headed over to the nightstand and picked up the phone he'd muted. "What?"

Pierre responded, "A courier should be arriving within the next five minutes with the Stradivarius. I would like to speak to my daughter."

"So would I," Harbinger said and hung up the phone. He put his earpiece in and tapped it. "Courier inbound with a violin."

"You know they put those old-fashioned Tommy Guns in violin cases, right?"

"You watch too much television," Harbinger told the techie.

"Is that possible? Television is my bestie. And I'm not stupid. I know the dimensions of a Tommy Gun and a violin are not compatible. The Tommy guns of that era were at least five and three-quarter inches longer than a standard violin."

Harbinger stopped and put his hands on his hips, watching Ysabel take slacks out of the closet and fold them into the suitcase. "How …"

"I have an IQ of 160. I'm not just a pretty face."

He blinked at that bit of information. "Noted. Let me know when the courier arrives," he said before putting the device back into listening mode.

Ysabel glanced at him. "Did I hear something about a violin?"

"Your father is sending a courier with your violin."

She blinked, and a smile spread across her face. "Really?"

"So he says." Harbinger wouldn't be surprised if it were a different one. He couldn't see the man expending the effort to locate and obtain the instrument or giving the expensive violin to

Ysabel. With what he'd learned about Pierre, there was always some kind of self-centered motivation.

"Hey, I can read the documents." Con's voice cracked in his ear again. Harbinger ignored it. "Damn, dude. There are ledger book pages here detailing payoffs to some pretty high-placed officials. Even in the United States. Hold on. Okay, I'm making huge leaps and not reading everything here. Oh, yes, there are bank accounts and addresses for each of the deposits. Hello … I know a couple of these people. They're black hat hackers. Wicked sharp. Dude, offshore accounts, no private Swiss accounts. Oh, lookie there. Nadia has her own little ventures going on. Hold on, let me check …"

Harbinger tapped his earpiece. "You do talk a lot."

"To myself when I'm working," Con admitted. "I think Nadia is siphoning or diverting money. It's a shell game. See the ball, under this cup, but surprise it didn't stay there, type of thing. She'd need one hell of a computer person to do that for her. Someone in … hold on, I'm following the dots …" Harbinger listened to a furious clacking of computer keys as Ysabel moved from the closet and dresser to the suitcase.

"This one or this one?" Ysabel held up two different dresses.

"Both."

Harbinger smiled at her when she rolled her eyes. "Not helpful. I have limited space."

"Then neither, add more lacy things. You know how much I like them."

"Dude, you're *not* muted," Con reminded him. "The source of the transfers is here in France. Oh shit. Dude, the IP address is in Pierre's building."

Harbinger sat up. "Meaning?"

"As I said, total and complete wild ass guess here, but maybe Nadia and Pierre are working together. I need to validate so much of this, but my gut says I'm not far off base. I could be wrong. I have to be. These transfers have been going on for, hell, three years, no—four."

"How has Molchalin not discovered this?" Harbinger was confused.

Con grunted. "Too much money? Who knows."

Harbinger didn't buy that rationale. He asked, "Would you have found the movement of monies if you didn't have the information in front of you?"

"Eventually, maybe, but like, do you hire accountants for illegal money, or do you just assume it's where you put it?"

"Good question. Are you sending this to CCS?"

"Of course. They're probably asleep, though. It's early over there." Con swore. "You've got a Vespa outside. Woman courier with a violin case."

Harbinger frowned. "A woman?"

"Fuck, dude, the Corsica goons are following her into the building. Two, no, three of them."

Harbinger grabbed Ysabel as she walked past him. "Come with me."

"What? What's happening?" Ysabel squeaked as she jogged with him down the hallway. Harbinger opened the guest bedroom door, marched through to the closet, and opened the comm room door.

"What is this?" Ysabel was looking everywhere at once.

He didn't have time to explain. "Later, I promise." He pointed at Con. "Do you have your weapon?"

"Always." Con's usual smart-ass demeanor vanished. "I've got her. Be careful."

"Always." He kissed Ysabel, gently pushed her into the room she'd never seen before, then shut the door after her. Three men, one woman. Nadia—it had to be Nadia—and the goons were her backup. She was who they were waiting for.

Harbinger jogged into the front room as a knock sounded.

He stopped, drew a deep breath, and opened the door. Nadia was there with a violin case. It was Ysabel's. He'd seen it enough to recognize the gray leather and red topstitching.

He also recognized the nine mil in Nadia's hand.

"Back up." Nadia's Russian accent was immediately discernable.

Three men rounded the corner at the sound of her voice. Harbinger held up his hands and backed into his apartment. Nadia's sneer reminded her of Smith's when he was pissed. Her hired goons walked in first, and she followed them. Nadia shut the door, and one at a time, her hired muscle screwed silencers onto their weapons. Nadia dropped the case, and it bounced onto its side. She kicked it toward the wall and moved in, looking around, seemingly taking in the grandeur of his apartment.

There was a similarity between her and Ysabel, but Nadia looked more like Smith than she did Ysabel. Her features were more masculine and hardened.

Nadia brought her attention back to him. "Where is she?"

Harbinger stepped back and to his right as one of the men moved through the apartment. "Not here." His eyes never stopped moving as he answered. He was assessing his enemies and looking for weaknesses. Nadia sighed and put her weapon down on the coffee table before sitting down and crossing her arms.

Harbinger moved again, putting his hands by his sides and centering his weight on the balls of his feet. He heard the man come back into the room.

"Clear," the Mafia muscle said from directly behind him.

Nadia made a tsking noise. "I didn't ask you where she wasn't. I asked you where she was. You'll learn the cost of wasting my time." She flicked her hand toward the largest of the men. The meat handed his weapon to the one who'd been behind Harbinger, bringing all three men into his view, which was perfect for his intent. When the Mafia muscle turned toward him, he was ready.

Harbinger smiled at the guy. He'd been storing one fuckton of a lot of aggression and was more than happy to take it out on those three amateurs. That caused the man to falter for just a second. It was all the time he needed. Striking out with his right foot, he smashed the side of the knee of the man holding two weapons. Harbinger felt bones and cartilage snap under the force of his kick and heard the crack as weapons clattered to the marble floor. The man cried out and fell. Harbinger's next strike was to the throat of the man approaching him. He hit hard enough to collapse the trachea. The big man grabbed his throat and dropped to his knees, rasping in a weird, breathless cough.

Harbinger launched toward Nadia, kicked her in the chest, which pushed her back into the couch. At the same time, he grabbed Nadia's weapon. The last man standing pointed his gun at Harbinger and fired. The bullet's song zapped past his ear, but the blast of Nadia's nine mil was the last thing the man would see because Harbinger didn't miss. The bullet Harbinger fired entered the man's skull just a fraction above his eyes. The man fell backward into the spattered remains of his brain.

Harbinger unloaded the nine mil and dropped the magazine and bullet from the chamber before turning back to Nadia. Harbinger kicked the other weapons away from Mr. No Knee as he followed her. The woman scrambled on her hands and knees toward the front door.

He grabbed the back of her shirt and lifted her up. She scratched and clawed at him with her nails and tried to bite him, screaming obscenities in Russian. Harbinger grabbed her by the throat and pushed her against the door, squeezing hard enough to silence her. "Con, take care of the police response."

"On it."

The woman quieted. In Russian, she hissed, "He will kill you."

Harbinger glanced over at the men on the floor. One was dead, one was dying, and the other was lying in a heap, moaning. He turned back to her. In perfect Russian, he responded, "Your father doesn't scare me."

"No, you fucking idiot. Pierre. He will kill you for touching me." She sneered at him. "Abrasha will kill you if Pierre fails. But he won't fail."

"Your *uncle* isn't that concerned, I assure you."

"He isn't my uncle. He and my mother were adopted from different families. He is not blood relation."

Harbinger's fingers tightened against the woman's throat. He connected the dots. Pierre and

Nadia were together. Nadia assumed the man would be her knight in shining armor. But Pierre didn't give a shit about anyone but Pierre. A lesson Nadia would soon learn, no doubt. "Still not concerned. You're dead, and so is Pierre. Your father will kill you. I've seen the documents your mother gave Ysabel."

All the color in Nadia's face drained. "That is a lie. She didn't take anything."

"No, she didn't *take* anything. She copied everything and had it laser inscribed on a ring that was in the envelope. Hundreds of pages of documentation, including payoffs to well-placed government officials, even in the United States. Imagine how mad your father will be when his people are arrested."

Nadia licked her lips, and her eyes darted everywhere but at him. Harbinger added, "I know you're double-crossing your father, Nadia. How long do you think it'll take before he finds out and kills you and Pierre?"

Nadia, eyes wide with fear, looked up at him. *Bingo.* The woman was in bed with Pierre, and they were definitely screwing over her father and, from the feeling he got, each other. She grabbed his hand around her neck and tried to pry it away.

He squeezed just a bit harder. She panted, trying to breathe. "He won't believe you."

"Evidence is hard to deny, and unless you tell me everything you know about Pierre Archambeau and this crypto heist, he's going to blame you." His fingers squeezed a little tighter.

"And if I talk?"

"If it's the truth, *I* won't kill you today." Harbinger stared at the woman, letting her know he wasn't joking. She licked her lips again and shook her head. "You have to protect Pierre and me. You have to hide us. My father has eyes everywhere."

"Except Pierre's bedroom?" Harbinger lifted an eyebrow.

"He knows. He doesn't care." She stopped trying to pry his fingers away from her throat. "I have your promise you'll protect us?"

"No." Harbinger stared at the woman. She wasn't getting any protection from him. Not after what she and Pierre had done to Ysabel. "*You* talk, or *I* kill you. I have the documents. I'm in control of this situation. Not you, not Pierre, not your father."

Nadia stared at him for a long time. "Pierre is stealing the money. Do you really love her?"

As if he'd chitchat with her about his love life. "How is he stealing the crypto?"

The woman almost smiled at his lack of answer, but she didn't. Instead, she said, "The program. I know nothing about it, but my father gave it to Pierre to use to gain access to the electronic keychains that hold the crypto. The program won't work against the chains because they aren't a firewall. They're a combination of numbers that it takes a supercomputer to defeat."

"Pierre is stealing all the money, even the money that is Abrasha's from this event?"

Nadia frowned. "What do you mean? All the money is being stolen at Abrasha's directive. There's a list of names Pierre is to target. Thirteen in total."

The fucker. Of course, Pierre didn't tell him the truth. Harbinger stared down at the woman. "How long have you been sleeping with Archambeau?"

"Does it matter? He's promised that when he gets this money, he and I will disappear, and I won't have to deal with my father again."

"When is the heist?"

The woman looked up and to the left before she lied. "I don't know."

Con's voice came over the device in his ear.

"Police have been diverted. Contacting Guardian about the mess in the front room."

Harbinger jerked the woman off the wall and turned her around. It took him less than a minute to pat her down and remove her cell phone and a small knife at her ankle. He switched to English, "Con, I need flexicuffs. There's a go-bag in the far-right corner of the room. Let CCS know there's one here for interrogation." He grabbed her arm and moved her away from the front door.

Walking through a vase that shattered from the bullet that missed him, Nadia stepped over the dead man as if he were a bump on the sidewalk. She didn't flinch or glance at the man, who was now passed out from the pain of a shattered knee. "I have more information. If you promise to protect Pierre and me from him. I will tell you, but you'll never get extradition or a conviction for my father. Too many people owe him."

Con walked out into the living room. "Here." He handed Harbinger two large flexicuffs. "I figured you'd want to make sure she wouldn't try to run away."

"Good idea." Harbinger put the flexicuffs on the woman. As he finished, Con's hand landed on his shoulder. "I've got her. You've got another problem to deal with. We have a team inbound to help take out the trash. I'll wait for them."

"Thanks." Harbinger checked Nadia's restraints and stood up.

"The powers that be are up to date. The team will be here shortly."

"Got it. Her phone." He tossed the device to Con, who popped open the back and pulled out the battery. He lifted the phone and showed it to Harbinger. "Same tracker."

"Tracker?" Nadia's eyes bounced between the two of them. "That can't be. These are clean phones."

Con snorted. "Yeah? Who told you that? Daddy Dearest?" Con reached into his pocket, pulled out a knife, and pried the gold square away from the base of the phone. He handed it to Harbinger. "You know where that goes."

"Done." He grabbed the tracker and went back to the comm room. He opened the door, and Ysabel launched herself at him. "I thought you were going to be killed. They all had guns. The vase shattered. He shot at you!"

Harbinger held her tightly as he reached for the Faraday box and dropped the tracker into it along with the one Pierre had in his phone. He then wrapped his arms around her and rocked her until she pulled away.

"I watched everything. You were so fast." Ysabel's hands were shaking against his chest. "You shot him." She closed her eyes. "But he was going to kill you. I saw him trying to point the gun at you when you were moving ... and then the vase ... then your gun ... He could have killed you."

"I'm fine." He pulled her in for another hug.

"This is what you do. Your security job. You hunt these people, right?" She arched her back so she could look up at him.

"My responsibilities are more than just hunting people who are dangerous, but at the base of it, what you saw me do today is what can happen when I am called to work," Harbinger told her as much as he, in good conscience, could.

She turned and looked at the monitor. "I tried to get out when I saw the guns. I tried to come to help you, but Con stopped me. He told me you were one of the best in the world at what you do. Then I saw ..." She blinked rapidly and shook her head. Pulling a shaking breath, she lifted her eyes and looked at him. "You could have protected me. Eight months ago, when my father convinced me to leave you. Being with you was the safest place I could be."

"It was and always will be." Harbinger wrapped his arms around her as she leaned into him.

Ysabel turned her head toward the monitor. "Is that my sister?"

"That's Nadia, but you don't have to claim her as a sister. She's never treated you like one."

Ysabel nodded. "What did you say to her? Were you speaking Russian?"

"We were. I was asking her questions."

"Did she answer?"

"She did, but I don't know how much to believe." The woman had caved a bit too early and too easily. Someone as hardened as Nadia ... a person who could step over dead bodies without missing a beat, was someone he didn't expect to spew out information the way she had. It was counterintuitive. Harbinger believed her words to be a well-planned scheme at best and a set-up at worst. He was hedging his bets and putting all his chips on the scheme *and* set-up. And he'd put Pierre behind all of it.

"I don't want to leave you, but honestly, I can't wait to get on the plane." Ysabel sighed heavily. "You'll be safe, right?"

"You know I will be. I have too much waiting for me at home not to take every precaution." He squeezed her a bit as they hugged and rocked back and forth.

"Jinx is inbound to sit on that bitch, so your damn techie can continue to get us information off that flat. Harbinger, we've bumped the departure of the aircraft. A car will be outside your door in five minutes. Get her to the airstrip." Fury's voice disturbed the quiet connection between him and Ysabel.

"The name's Con." Con chuckled, and Fury growled.

Harbinger stopped rocking and realized he hadn't silenced his communications device. So everyone and their brother had heard what Ysabel and he had said to each other. Well, fuck it. At least he wouldn't have to repeat it in his report. "I copy. We'll leave as soon as Jinx gets here."

Ysabel blinked up at him, and he explained. "We're leaving as soon as someone gets here to watch Nadia. The plane's departure has been bumped up, and our car is on its way."

He took her by the hand and headed to the bedroom, purposefully walking between Ysabel and the sight in the living room. "I'm almost ready.

I just need the things from the bathroom. Anything else I can buy," Ysabel said to herself as she marched straight into the bathroom.

"I'm online, H. I'll talk with her on the way back to the States. I'll make sure she feels welcome and knows the job is off-limits."

"Thanks," he responded. "How's Smith?"

"Smith is fine," the man answered for himself.

"So he says," Val countered. "Does she know she's got a half-brother?"

"No." Harbinger hadn't sprung that on her yet.

"I can tell her," Smith replied. "Unless it's something you want to do."

"No, go for it," Harbinger said as she came out with an armful of bottles and pouches.

"And can I say for a moment there I thought Nadia and her uncle were doing the nasty." Val sighed.

Harbinger chuffed out a puff of air. "They are."

"Yeah, but they aren't blood relation, so it's less gross. Kind of. Maybe. Okay, still gross." Val made a shivering sound.

"The car is pulling up. Right behind the team." Jewell's voice broke into the conversation. "I burrowed into your security feed when Con took over watching Nadia. I didn't want any more unannounced surprises," she said by way of explanation.

"The car's here." Harbinger tapped his comm device into listen mode and helped her zip up her suitcase.

She grabbed her purse and checked for her passport and the credit card he'd given her. "I can use my own." She handed it back to him.

He shook his head. "If you use your card, it's a way someone can track you. I'd rather you use this for any purchase until we get everything sorted." He folded it back into her hand. "Besides, I'd want to replace all that fancy lace I've ruined along the way."

She smiled for a moment and then put the card back into her purse. "Only so you can ruin it again."

Harbinger lifted his eyebrows a couple of times. "Definitely." They laughed together before he took her hand in his and lifted her suitcase. "I want you to stare straight forward when we walk through the living room. Just look at the door, not Nadia, not Con, and not the men on the floor. There are also several other people in the front room." He'd heard the team announce their arrival.

"Hey, anyone, can you verify a really big, really

pissed-off-looking man named Jinx is supposed to be here?" That was the female member of the security team.

"I can," Fury said. "He has a scar running from his little finger to his elbow on his right arm. He's there to take over watching that bitch."

"Good. I was going to clock her if I had to listen to her mouth any longer," the woman said.

"Giovanni, since you're there, you can interrogate her for us." Fury chuckled. "Have Jinx in the room with you when you do it."

"Plausible deniability. I didn't kill her. He did."

A deep, resonating voice came across the line. "No, she killed her. I didn't."

Fury snorted. "I think you two will work well together."

"What information am I getting?"

"Anything you can," Fury said. "Release the hounds."

"Done."

Harbinger interrupted. "Outbound."

"Come out. I've checked the violin case. There's a violin in there and three trackers. I've eliminated all of them." A new voice.

He glanced at Ysabel. "Ready?"

She nodded, and he opened the bedroom door.

As they moved into the living room, Spike came out from under the couch, and one of the team members scooped him up. "We'll take care of him until you're back."

"Thanks," Ysabel said at the same time as Harbinger. Harbinger was impressed with the team. Black plastic sheets covered the two dead men, and the medic was working on the unconscious one. Harbinger nodded at who he assumed was Jinx. The man stood to the side, silent as a sentinel, but he knew the look. Jinx dipped his chin in return.

Nadia started to spew cuss words in French at Ysabel. The woman standing in front of her reached out and slapped the shit out of Nadia. "Manners," she reprimanded.

Ysabel glanced at Nadia and then at Harbinger. Her eyes were wide, and the slightest hint of a smile flashed across her face. Harbinger winked at his fiancée. She took her violin case from one of the team members on the way out the door.

They were followed down the stairs by the same man who had held the case for her, and he watched over them until they were inside the limo. Harbinger put up the security screen and made sure his comm was turned to listen only.

Ysabel looked at him, and she narrowed her eyes. "I wanted to slap her. Such language!"

Harbinger chuckled and diverted the conversation. "Check the violin."

She pulled the case closer to her and opened it. Taking the instrument out, her fingers caressed the wood, and she lifted it to examine it. "There's a new scratch here in the purfling and a small ding here near the saddle." She plucked each of the four strings. "G, D, A, and E." She frowned and twisted a tuning peg and then plucked the last string again. "She's fine." Ysabel smiled at him. "Thank you for getting her back for me."

"She's part of you. I'm just surprised he surrendered it. It's valuable."

"And mine." Ysabel nodded. "I own it. He didn't make it to my first performance as first chair. I didn't expect him to, really. He rarely showed up for any of my milestone events. He apologized and told me I could have anything I wanted. I told him I wanted him to legally transfer the violin to me. I have the papers in a safety deposit box."

Harbinger cocked his head. "Why?"

"I hate to admit it, but somewhere inside, I knew he didn't care for me the way a father cares for a child. Things people said as I grew up. The fact I was in the United States for four years at school, and he never came to see me. He was controlling but distant." She shrugged. "All the things that didn't quite make sense then do now. I often wondered why he didn't marry. I guess his mistresses were enough."

"Perhaps." Harbinger doubted the man could pretend to love someone long enough to marry them. "I believe he has psychopathic tendencies."

"What do you mean?" Ysabel asked as she placed her violin into the case.

He shrugged. "He manipulates people, has a complete disregard for anyone but himself, no apparent empathy, and he has yet to speak the absolute truth to either of us. Yet he's able to maintain an appearance of a normal life."

Ysabel leaned back in the seat and nodded. "That makes a lot of sense." She sighed. "And still …"

"You love him."

"I do." She nodded. "He's my father."

"And that's another reason I love you. Your love is deep, and it's true."

She leaned into him, and they rode in silence for several minutes. "You killed those men."

"I did." She witnessed it; there was no need to deny what happened.

"It was easy for you, wasn't it?"

"Easy? To take a life? No." He always weighed the crime the individual committed against his legislated punishment. If he ever doubted, even for a second, the Council was wrong, he'd walk, and he'd made that abundantly clear.

"No, I mean …" She shook her head. "The way you did it. The training, you were swift, and everything you did was with precision. You hit notes that others can't. Ahhggg." She lifted her hands in the air. "I don't know how to say it, but you're …"

"Skilled."

"Yes!" She slapped her thighs. "Yes, skilled. You've practiced these moves." She jabbed out in front of her.

"All the time," he admitted.

"Can you teach me?"

He frowned. "Why?"

She turned and blinked at him. "Because I never want to be in a prison with a rat again." She shivered. "A rat, Heath." She put her hands out in front of her. "That big. If you teach me, I can defend myself."

He took her hand in his. The prison and the rat were all on her father. That bastard had orchestrated everything. He knew it, and Nadia had confirmed it. Pierre, his colleagues, and Nadia were her only threats. He hoped to eliminate each from her life in one fashion or the other. "I can teach you, but some of the work is hard on the hands." He lifted hers to his lips and kissed them. "I would never forgive myself if you were injured and couldn't play. How about I teach you what I can without compromising your music and promise that, for the rest of my life, I will protect you and keep you from harm?"

She stared at him and smiled. "For the rest of my life."

He tapped her ring. "When I get back, we'll get married. Plan any type of wedding you want."

She shook her head. "I don't want a big wedding. I just want to marry you. The wrapping isn't important. What we are is."

"Then we'll find a judge and get married as soon as I get home." The car slowed down, and he looked out the window. He could see the shiny black jet Guardian had sent for her, Val, and Smith.

When Ysabel tapped him on the shoulder, he turned back to her. "As soon as you get home, I expect you to damage more lace."

Harbinger moved in one motion, pushing her back until she was prone. "I love you. Never question it. Never doubt it."

"I know, and I will never doubt it. I love you, Heath." She pushed his hair back from his brow. "Come to me when this is done." He lowered and kissed her with the emotion lodged in every fiber of his being. When the car stopped, he lifted away. "We're here."

Ysabel sighed. "Heaven? I agree."

He chuckled and helped her sit up. "There's Val and Smith." Another vehicle approached. He turned back to her. "It's time."

He opened the door and stepped out while the driver retrieved Ysabel's suitcase. She handed him her violin, and he held her hand as she exited the vehicle. It was time, but damn it, he didn't want to be separated from her again. And yet she'd be safer with Val while he and Guardian tried to unscramble the web of deceit Pierre had spun around them. It was time to do his job, even if it meant taking out the father of the woman he loved.

CHAPTER 18

Ysabel reluctantly let go of Heath's hand at the bottom of the steps leading to the private jet. "You'll be exceptionally careful, yes?" She touched his cheek. The warmth and roughness of his stubble against her fingertips felt as familiar as the press of the strings against the neck of her violin. She loved both sensations, but nothing would ever equal the way she felt about Heath. If anyone asked her to decide between him and her music, she would gladly give up her violin for the rest of her life.

"That's a promise. As soon as I'm done here, I'll come for you." His hands landed on her hips. "Val and Smith are good people. You'll be safe with them." He leaned down and took her lips with a kiss that reached her soul and claimed her for eternity. When he pulled away, he stared down at her. "I love you."

"I'll never doubt it." She toed up and kissed him briefly. "You are my life." She stared at him. "My love for you is forever."

"Guys, I'm really sorry to break up the farewell, but someone needs to sit down," Val said from behind Heath. She spun and glanced at Smith. The big guy was pale.

"Damn, need help?" Heath reached for Smith.

Smith straightened a bit, wincing as he did. "I can climb a flight of stairs."

"You can catch him when he falls backward," Val said, motioning Heath after her husband. She glanced at Ysabel's violin case. "Whatcha got there?" She pointed at the case.

"My Stratovarius." Ysabel lifted it a bit.

"You play?" Val looked from her to Heath and Smith, who were halfway up the stairs.

"A little." Ysabel smiled.

"She's the best in the world," Heath said with his hand on Smith's back. "Steady there, big guy. I don't want to become a tarmac pancake."

"Fuck you," Smith retorted breathlessly.

"See, I told you he wasn't feeling well." Val

looked at Ysabel. "He rarely cusses in front of a lady."

Smith stopped at the top of the stairs and turned carefully. "My apologies." He nodded before Heath encouraged him into the cabin.

"Should he be traveling?" Ysabel walked to the stairs with Val.

"Oh, he'll be okay. Like all men, he just thinks he's invincible." They started up the stairs together. "Guardian wouldn't risk his health. The doctor is going back to the States with us because he's being reassigned. Most of our medical providers rotate in and out of countries. They get to travel and see the world, and we get the best medical care available."

Ysabel placed her violin and purse by one of the large chairs. "Guardian is that big?"

"Honey, Guardian is global." Val laughed. "Go say goodbye to your fiancé, and I'll get Smith settled before the doctor gets here." Val headed to the back of the plane.

Ysabel smiled at Heath as he approached. "I wasn't planning on coming on the aircraft. I guess we get another goodbye kiss." He wrapped his arms around her and leaned down.

Ysabel molded into his firm body. She wanted

to memorize everything about the moment. His smell, his taste, the feel of his body against hers. He lifted away too soon, but then again, forever wasn't enough time with him. "I'll come for you as soon as I'm done."

She nodded. "Until then, my love."

"Until then." He moved away, releasing her hand only when he was too far away to keep a grip. It was his way, and it was an action that showed her over and over again how much he loved her.

Heath moved to the side, and another man and a pilot entered the aircraft. "Hey, Doc. Long time."

"H. No stitches needed today?"

"Nah, I'm good. Enjoy the flight." He winked at Ysabel, then jogged down the stairs.

The doctor nodded at her and went to the back of the aircraft. The pilot extended his hand to her. "The name's Mackenzie, but you can call me Mack. I'm your pilot for the trip. My copilot is finishing the preflight, and then we'll be going. If there's anything we can do for you during the flight, just let us know. Back there's the galley. It's self-serve and completely stocked. You'll need to be seated and belted in during take-off and landing. The chairs are equipped with a shoulder and lap harness and flotation devices are in a compartment under the chair. You won't need them, but regulations say I have to tell you where they are. The others have flown with us so many times they know the drill."

Ysabel nodded. "My violin?"

"Yeah, it should be stowed, but that looks like an expensive case. You can strap it in the chair over here." He pointed to a smaller chair beside the table.

"Thank you." She moved over and strapped in her case. By the time she was done, both the doctor and Val were back.

"He's a stubborn man." The doctor sat down and strapped himself in. "But most of the Guardians I've met are." The doctor looked over to her. "I'm Zeb Frazier."

"Ysabel Archambeau," she introduced herself. "Is Smith okay?"

"He will be. He's pushing too hard."

"He's not a fan of admitting any weakness," Val said with a shrug as the doctor made a noise of agreement.

The copilot came in, raised the steps, and closed the door behind him. He rubbed his hands together as he walked to the flight deck. "We'll be taxiing in just a minute." He motioned to Ysabel. "Please strap in."

"Oh, sorry." It took only a few seconds for her to sit down and strap in. The engines whined shortly thereafter, and they were off the ground faster than she expected.

After they leveled and the seat belt sign was extinguished, Val was out of her seat. "He'll be up and out of that bed … See? You can't keep him down."

The doctor rolled his eyes and grabbed a paperback out of his briefcase. "I'll be here when the stitches start to bleed."

Val made a face and then turned to her. "Come on back and visit with us." Ysabel glanced at the couch where Smith was now sitting. She unbuckled and followed Val back to the small seating area.

"Why didn't you sit in the seats for takeoff?" Ysabel asked Smith.

"Surgical incision. The chest harness would have caused discomfort. How are you doing? I understand the morning was … eventful."

Ysabel drew a deep breath. "Very. Heath handled everything, and Con kept me from running into the front room to try to help him.

When I saw what he was capable of … I've made so many mistakes."

Smith and Val exchanged a look. "H isn't one of those mistakes," Val said defensively.

Her eyes snapped to Val so quickly it almost hurt. "No, he isn't. The mistakes were telling him I didn't love him and forcing him away from me when I was in trouble. He could've prevented all this from happening. I should have trusted my instincts, but I let my father convince me *I* was protecting *him*." Ysabel shook her head. "If I'd only known."

Val leaned forward. "You weren't supposed to know. No one is. What we do is highly classified. When we get to the States, you'll meet the rest of our team. They do the same type of things as we do, in different areas and with different skill sets, but no one will ever mention work. We get together, have fun, celebrate, and sometimes, we mourn, but we never talk about the job."

Ysabel stared at her. "If that was a warning, I understand. What happened this morning opened my eyes, and I assume I know what the job entails." She looked down for a moment before leaning forward on her elbows and staring at Val. "I watched the man I love fight for his life and mine.

What he did was necessary. I don't know you or the others, but I know Heath. He'd never do anything that wasn't absolutely necessary. I know his heart. He's a good man." She pressed her hand over her heart. "His job, as far as I'm aware, is a consultant for a global company. He's a troubleshooter for management issues. Are you suggesting there's some other job he does?"

Val smiled and leaned back into her husband's side. "Nope. I think you've got the job description down."

Smith smiled at her. "I understand you've found out your biological father is Abrasha Molchalin."

Ysabel flopped back into her chair. "That's what I'm told." She shook her head. "My supposed sister was at the apartment this morning. I don't think I want to be associated with that bloodline."

Smith looked at Val, who put her hand on his leg and nodded. "I believe I understand your sentiment and distaste."

Ysabel shook her head. "I don't know if you could. From what I've gathered, both of them, Abrasha and Nadia, are criminals."

Smith waited until she looked at him again. "Abrasha is my father, or so we believe."

Ysabel blinked and looked from Val, who was nodding, back to the massive man in front of her. "Then ... we're related?"

"Supposedly," he admitted. "We've been unable to validate it. No one has Abrasha's DNA."

Ysabel pointed to herself. "But I do. If what you say is true, we should share DNA, right?"

Smith nodded. "Yes."

"Then we'll take a test. If we have the same father, it should be evident." Ysabel looked at the man who could be her brother. He'd given her the shirt off his back, was shot trying to help her, and worked for an organization she'd come to respect. "You, I'd be honored to be related to."

Smith smiled again. That time, it was a beaming smile that transformed his face. "And I you."

"Your mother? She couldn't tell you anything about him?"

Smith looked up at the ceiling of the aircraft. "That's a story for when I'm feeling a bit better. Suffice to say my parents were and still are ..."

"Troglodytes and assholes," Val supplied.

Smith chuffed out a laugh. "That."

"Tell me about the violin," Val said. "I've always wanted to play an instrument, but I'm tone-deaf."

Ysabel laughed. "You're not."

Smith's eyes shot up. He looked at his wife and then back at her. "She is."

"Hey!" Val leaned away from him. "You're not supposed to agree."

"I love when you sing in the shower or in the car or when you're happy." Smith smiled at her. "But you can't carry a tune in a bucket."

Val stared at her husband and narrowed her eyes at him before bursting into laughter. "I'd be mad at you if it weren't true." She glanced over at Ysabel. "How long have you played?"

"As long as I can remember. My nanny gave me a child's violin when I was four. She played and gave me lessons. When I was five, she suggested to my father he embrace my talent and hire teachers for me. I outgrew the instructors who could be brought to my boarding school, so my father arranged for me to go to Juilliard when I was old enough. Since a high school degree wasn't necessary to attend, they base admissions on talent only; I lived in the United States for four years with a host family my father paid."

"H said you were the best in the world," Smith said.

"I'm not. I'm good, and I love music, but there

are others who far eclipse my mastery." She smiled at them. "I think Heath may be a bit biased." She cocked her head and then asked, "Why do you call him H?"

"Ah, that's just a work thing. Several of our coworkers have weird names they go by. Ice, Malice, and Flack. Names they got during training that we've always called them." Val chuckled. "Wives are not required to call them by their nicknames."

"How long have you worked together?" Ysabel wanted to know more about Heath.

"Wow." Val's brow furrowed. "It seems like forever. Training took years. Then we were put in the field. Anyway, we've been friends forever. Harbinger is a wonderful person. When he gets back to the States, we're going to have to help him find a house near the rest of us in Virginia. I can't wait to show you our house. Smith remodeled it for me into a little piece of heaven."

"Close to shopping and far enough away from everybody who needs to call before they come over." Smith smiled. "Those were the two requirements I had to fulfill."

"And you did it." She leaned in and kissed his

cheek. Pulling back, she put her hand on his brow. "You're warm."

"I'm ready to rest for a bit." Smith nodded. "I don't need the doctor, but I do know my limits."

"Wait." Val twisted and pointed at Ysabel. "You heard that, right? He admitted he has limits."

Ysabel nodded. "I heard it."

With Val's help, Smith carefully stood up and went to the back of the plane. Ysabel went back to the front and unstrapped her violin. "Would it bother you if I played?" she asked the doctor.

He glanced up at her and blinked. "No, not at all. I'd enjoy it ... unless you're going to play square dance music. 'Turkey in the Straw' is not my favorite."

She laughed. "No, I was thinking Paganini or perhaps Bach."

The doctor smiled. "Please, I'd be honored."

Ysabel took out her Stradivarius and her E. Sartory original bow. She carefully inspected it, tightened it, and rosined the hair. Once again, she listened carefully to the notes as she plucked the strings and tightened or loosened the pegs as needed before she tucked the violin and drew the bow across the strings.

She closed her eyes and played the music in

her soul. The songs moved from one to another. Her fingers danced along the strings as she drew her bow, forming the tones that delivered her to another place. For her, playing wasn't about the mechanics. It was about the heart. The leap from knowing the notes to hit to delivering a rhapsody of emotion and love was one she willingly took. Besides being in Heath's arms, this metamorphosis, emboldened by the works of the masters, was the only other place she felt so alive and complete.

When she ended her last song, she opened her eyes. The doctor, Smith, Val, and the pilot named Mack were situated around her.

"That was the most beautiful thing I've ever heard." Val had tears in her eyes. "H was right. You are the best in the world."

Ysabel smiled as she lowered her violin. "Thank you, but there are better."

"You couldn't prove it by me," the pilot said, getting up. "Thank you for that. It was amazing."

"That was not 'Turkey in the Straw'," the doctor said.

Ysabel laughed. "I could play it for you."

"God, no." The doctor laughed.

"I thought you were going to rest." Ysabel

looked at Smith, who was reclining on the couch. "Did I bother you?"

He shook his head. "The music was wonderful. I rested here where I could hear you. Thank you."

Ysabel could feel herself blushing. "It's been a while since I could play." Time where she wondered if she'd ever be able to play again. But both of her loves were restored to her. Heath and her music. There was nothing else she could ask for.

CHAPTER 19

Harbinger bolted from the car into his building. The chatter in his ear had been nonstop, and things seemed to be moving fast. When he opened the door, the first thing he noticed was a lack of bodies on the floor.

"That was quick."

"Nah, not really. We're just tidy. The dead ones are on ice until tonight, and then we'll move them. The injured one died of shock, we think, or his heart gave out. But you've got a clean sweep. There are no witnesses except the woman." The man who'd followed him and Ysabel to the car earlier extended his hand. "I'm Ranger, team skipper. That's Giovanni, best damn interrogator in the world. Over there with the comm pack is Radar.

He's got that sense of when shit is going to happen, like the guy on the old sitcom. Our medic and explosives expert, Crash, is over there, and our entry specialist, Dock."

"Don't they have their call signs switched?" Harbinger asked as he shook hands with each of the team members. "Nah, Crash hasn't met a vehicle he can't demolish, and Dock's name is actually Docker, so we shortened it."

"Where are we at?" he asked when he saw Con come into the front room.

"Boss man wants you to check in for a conference. Ranger and Jinx, too." Con headed into the kitchen. "But I'm getting some food first. No breakfast, past lunch. How does anyone expect me to pound the keyboard when my blood sugar dips."

"He talks a lot," Jinx said as he exited the kitchen with Spike in his arms. The cat seemed to be asleep as Jinx stroked the animal's fur. "Nice cat."

"Try having Con live with you. He talks nonstop, and thanks. I rescued Spike from a trio of trash who were torturing him when he was about five weeks old."

"Fuckers. Did you end them?" Jinx leveled a glare at him.

"They won't be messing with kittens any longer." Harbinger rubbed the back of his neck. "Did you get information from Nadia?" He looked around. "Where is she?"

"Tied up in the bathroom," Giovanni said. "She's a mean girl with some inflated sense of self-worth. Seems her boyfriend is going to kill me, and if he fails, she's sure her father will complete the mission."

"I got the same threat," Harbinger told her. "I'm shaking in my boots."

"I can tell. Well, doll face is on ice for a while. I'll chip away at her, but she needs to marinate before I roast her." Giovanni walked over and stroked Spike's fur. "Ranger, I think we need a team cat."

Ranger snorted. "Nope. But I'd give my left nut for one of those bomb dogs."

Giovanni snorted, "That would be cool, too. You giving up your nut, I mean. You're all the horndog we need on this team." The rest of the team busted up laughing. The woman winked at Jinx, although no one but Harbinger could see the interaction.

Con exited the kitchen with a full baguette, a package of cheese, a plateful of prosciutto, and two bottles of water. "Let's go." He headed into the comm room.

Harbinger let the others go first, then followed them into the secure area. He shut the door behind him and moved to one of the vacant seats.

"Sitrep," Archangel said as soon as they signed in.

"Three dead. Nadia is on ice, according to the interrogator. Smith, Val, the doctor, and Ysabel are in the air heading your way." Harbinger started his report. "I had a discussion with Nadia this morning after her men tried to kill me. I don't know how much of what she said was true, but based on the information Con was able to get from the documents and her immediate reaction, she and Pierre are stealing from Abrasha. Nadia said Pierre had a program that could go through firewalls but not the chains on the crypto. Something about needing a supercomputer to break through."

"Yeah, we have experience trying to break those types of passwords. Does he have access to a supercomputer?" Jewell asked from her panel in the video squares.

"Yep," Con replied. "Confirmation email from the French government about an hour ago. I did some digging. He bought it on the auspice of allowing the French government to use the system. He's been granted a license to run one and is charging huge amounts of money for the French establishments to use it."

"In the meantime, he uses it to break the crypto chains and steal money," Archangel said. "Have we determined the location he's setting up?"

"Yes," Jinx said and nodded to Con, who hit a few keys. A map popped onto the screen as Jinx continued, "The uninterrupted power supply needed for the system he'll be using has been installed here, and there's three-sixty security on sight. Cameras, alarm systems, and armed guards inside the facility. Generators are in the back, and there are three Dobies running free inside the enclosure. Nice dogs."

"Did you stop to pet them?" Fury sneered.

"Actually, yes, I did. I like animals more than I like people." Harbinger could believe it. Spike only cuddled with Ysabel, and yet he was asleep in Jinx's arms. "I believe they're close, if not finished, with the installation of equipment. There are no work trucks and no installations happening. Without breaking in, I can't guarantee it, but my gut is telling me it'll be soon."

"You said there was a surveillance camera?" Con interrupted.

"Yes, I did," Jinx answered in that precise manner of his.

Con put down his sandwich. "Jewell?"

"Yep, let's do it." Con wiped his fingers and started typing. "Hopefully, it isn't fiber."

Ranger looked confused. "What isn't fiber?"

"The camera system," Jacob King answered before adding, "Hang around them enough, and you start deciphering the language."

"The firewall is scalable," Jewell said as she and Con continued to type.

"Yeah, hold on, try this." Con's fingers flew across the keyboard.

"Great, yeah, that'll work…"

"We're in." Con hit a couple of keys, and the screen changed into a grid of video feeds.

"Any chance of them knowing you're monitoring?" Archangel asked.

"Always, but we're damn good," Con replied.

"Look, there's people working in that room. Second square down." Jacob pointed to the screen he was viewing.

"Hold on." Jewell made the picture bigger. "Five stations. We were right." Jewell chuckled. "Only two are at their stations right now. When they leave, we can try to get in. I don't want anyone to be online and figure out what we're doing."

"That would allow you to reroute the money?" Archangel wanted clarification.

"No, but it would allow us to monitor where money is going, and once it's deposited, we hack that institution and bounce it out," Con replied.

"So, you said all those words to say yes," Fury growled.

Con looked up at the camera and smiled before answering, "Yeah, basically."

Fury rolled his eyes so hard Harbinger swore he could hear the motion over the video feed. Harbinger tried not to laugh. Con was unique, but the man was a freaking genius. He could live with his mouth for the support Con gave to the mission. Fury turned his attention elsewhere. "Jinx, do you have a way in?"

"Yes, through the back. The door to the dog area is alarmed, but it isn't active. They think it is, but I disabled it by looping the power and disabling the sensors."

"There isn't a camera for the back," Jewell said.

"There could be," Con answered. "Panel fourteen isn't active."

"There is a camera, but by staying behind the generator and vehicles, there's a four- to five-foot gap we'd have to span to gain access." Jinx continued to stroke Spike. The cat was flat out on his back, paws up in the air, head hanging off Jinx's arm, and sound asleep. The guy had a way with animals; that was for sure.

"Movement on Pierre?"

Harbinger blinked and then bolted forward. "Shit, boss, I have a source who was supposed to get me information on Pierre's movement within the criminal element of the city. With everything that happened, I haven't called him back."

"Not like you haven't had enough on your plate. We're still ahead of the bastard, but get that information for us. CCS, get into that system. I want everything in place for when this goes down. We'll meet again in six hours."

"Rog-O," Jewell chimed in.

"On it," Con said at the same time.

"Ranger, do you need help taking out the trash?" Jacob asked before Archangel could end the call.

"Nah, we'll handle it. Not our first dumpster run."

"Make sure Con validates there are no cameras where you're dumping," Jewell said distractedly.

"Cool. Less driving around for us." Ranger fist-bumped Con. "What do you want done with the woman?"

"Turn Giovanni loose," Fury snapped.

"Nadia is a wanted person because of her association with her father and his alleged actions in conjunction with the Rostova group. We're detaining her for the proper authorities. I've officially requested to be *that* authority from our French and Swiss government liaisons. Fortunately, the French want nothing to do with Abrasha, and the Swiss have deferred jurisdiction to us for the Rostova incident, so I feel confident we'll be transporting her back to the States. Between Jared and Giovanni, we'll get the information we need." Archangel crossed his arms. "Our focus now is on this crypto heist and gathering as much information about Abrasha and Pierre as possible. The more ammo we have, the better."

Fury asked, "Has Archambeau become a person of interest outside this situation?"

"Unknown at this time." Archangel hedged on his answer, but that was fine by Harbinger. He knew the bastard was shady as fuck. "The names listed by Pierre are probably all lies, but he did make a mistake. Several of the names are United States citizens. Again, we're asking for primary jurisdiction because our company is the only entity with the intel, technology, and people in place to act immediately."

Archangel looked at the screen. "Anything else?"

"Pierre might come looking for Nadia." Harbinger shrugged. "I don't think he'd tip his hand that way, but she thinks they're a couple."

Archangel blinked. "A couple? His niece?"

"According to Nadia, they're not related by blood. Léonie and Pierre were adopted and not siblings," Con said. A set of birth certificates flashed on the screen. "Adopted, as Nadia said."

Archangel took off his glasses and shook his head. "And still, things surprise me. You'd think I've seen it all. Anyway, deal with him if he shows up. He can't know we're working on the crypto issue. I want him to make a grab for the money. Catching him in the act only bolsters our case against him and gets us closer to Abrasha. Removing Abrasha's money is poking the bear. I need a damn sharp stick. I want that bear mad enough to make mistakes."

"I copy." Harbinger leaned back in his chair.

"Anything else?" Archangel waited for a moment. "Six hours. Archangel is clear."

Harbinger listened to everyone sign out. "I need to make a call, gentlemen." Harbinger stood up, as did Ranger and Jinx.

"Con, we're going to take a drive around the city," Ranger said. "We'll give you the addresses as we pick them if you can check for cameras in the area."

"You got it."

Jinx turned to him. "If it's not an imposition, I'll stay and watch the woman for Giovanni."

"Not an imposition at all, and I appreciate it. Food and drink are in the kitchen." Harbinger looked at his cat and smiled, scratching the animal under the chin. Spike didn't move. "He's comatose."

"He was very stressed. Animals are astute, and the events in your home were not exactly Zen."

"Don't I know it?" Harbinger shut the door behind Jinx, then turned to Con, who'd just taken a huge bite of his sandwich. "You. No talking, no typing. Just eat. If this guy thinks someone else is in the room, I won't get shit."

Con's eyes widened, but he nodded and popped the top off a bottle of water.

Harbinger dialed Mathieu and put it on speaker. "Ah, my friend, you did not forget about me."

"Life became … complicated. Do you have the information I requested?"

"I do. This, of course, cannot be corroborated without due diligence on your part. Any action taken on my understanding of what is being said is … rumors."

"I'm not a cop, Mathieu, I don't give a fuck about evidence. I want to know what the son of a bitch is doing." Harbinger sat down and stared at the table. "Talk."

"Pierre Archambeau is an interesting man. He has a small army working for him. Recently, they were involved in an incident in the catacombs. People died."

"I am aware." And he wished like hell he'd been there for Smith. "What else do you have?"

"Drugs, girls, firearms, and blackmail. The scale is large."

"Running or receiving?"

"His army would never do anything but drive the car and transport the items from one place to another or perhaps deliver messages anonymously. Our friend is always one or two spaces removed from any possible repercussion."

"What kind of repercussions?"

"Russian and Corsican are the flavor of the day. There have been others, but not lately."

"Is he connected to Molchalin?"

There was a long pause at the other end of the phone. "Intimately, shall we say."

"His lover is Molchalin's daughter."

Mathieu chuckled. "Which makes things complicated. This woman is not in Molchalin's good graces. My sources in Russia tell me she was sent here for Archambeau to keep her out of trouble. She was caught going through his private office. If she wasn't related …"

"She'd be dead."

"An assumption, but based on history …" Mathieu let the sentence hang.

"Anything else?" Harbinger asked.

Again, Mathieu paused. "This will clear all debt I owe to you, correct?"

Harbinger assured him, "Yes, a clean slate."

"It's rumored Archambeau is working on something big. My people don't know what, but they know it'll happen very soon. *Very* soon. His people are absolutely silent about what's going on. That's all I know."

"Have a good life, Mathieu."

"Wish me a long life, my friend. Good is not in my nature."

Hanging up the phone, Harbinger glanced at Con. "Can you send that information to Archangel?"

Con nodded and finished chewing. "You have some interesting contacts. Dare I ask what favors he owed you for?"

"Not if you want to live." Harbinger stood up.

"Man, are all you Shadows in the habit of threatening people?" Con laughed as he wadded up his napkin and tossed it on the empty plate.

Harbinger clasped Con on the shoulder on his way out of the room. Con lifted his water bottle to his mouth as Harbinger spoke. "See, Con, you've misunderstood a basic principle. A shadow never threatens; we execute."

He couldn't help the smile as he shut the door on Con's coughing and sputtering.

CHAPTER 20

Harbinger stood in the kitchen and looked out the window as he listened to Ysabel's happy voice tell him about the flight, Smith, and being able to play for the first time in what felt like forever. "The house they live in is so nice. The bedroom is almost as big as your entire apartment and way bigger than the one I'd rented."

"Speaking of which, is there anything you want from your apartment?" He'd break in and get it for her after the mission.

There was silence for a moment. "No. The memories there are not what I want to start over. It's late there. I should let you go." Ysabel sighed. "I wish you were here."

"So do I, but it won't be long." He hoped. "You should take a nap and then try to adjust to it being morning instead of midnight." Which meant it was six in the morning on the East Coast.

"I will, but I wanted to talk to you before I did. I love you, Heath. Come to me when you can, and we'll start our life. One that doesn't include my past."

"I'm part of your past." Harbinger chuckled.

"No, you are my future, my present, and my love."

"I can live with that. I love you. Get some sleep."

Con's voice came over the comms. "H and Jinx, I need you in here now."

Ysabel sighed, "I will, good night."

"Sleep well." Harbinger ended the call as he hustled into the comm room. He met Jinx at the door.

"People, a fuckton of people, are arriving at the crypto heist location." Harbinger leaned forward at the same time as Jinx.

Harbinger pointed to the screen. "Teams. Shit, three, no, four teams. Get Ranger on the horn."

"I'm here," Ranger grunted before a crash was heard. "The last one is in the can. Literally."

"They have what looks like well-armed teams

deploying around the building. I count twenty." He looked at Jinx, who nodded in agreement.

"Sounds like a party. Con, can you pinpoint locations for us so we can deploy to our advantage?"

Jacob King's voice came online. "I have Delta team in the city. Ranger, you'll be lead. Delta Team Leader is still on medical restrictions."

"Copy. Con, find us a good rendezvous point, close but out of sight and hearing distance."

"Working it." Con was typing furiously.

"CCS online." Jewell's voice came through the speaker.

"The Rose is online." Fury sounded grumpier than usual.

"Archangel is online," Jewell said, and his unshaved image appeared on the video screen.

"Sitrep."

"It looks like it's going down," Harbinger replied. "Twenty men just pulled up in five SUVs and deployed around the area."

"All five stations are manned. And there's Pierre." Con pointed to another monitor.

"Were you able to get into the systems?" Jacob asked.

"Yes. As long as no one sweeps before they start, we should be good," Jewell answered.

"H and Jinx, get over there. I want Pierre taken into custody as soon as this event happens."

"Custody?" Jinx's surprised question mimicked Harbinger's own raised eyebrows.

"At this time, yes. Now, move," Archangel barked.

Harbinger had never heard the man lift his voice like that. He started out the door but shouted to Con. "You have Nadia. She's secure. Just don't let her out of her restraints for any reason. Jinx, with me." He ran through the apartment, opened his weapons safe, and pointed to his closet. "Clothes."

The men threw on tactical garb and armed up. "I have a vehicle outside." Jinx grabbed his keys.

"Let's go." Harbinger grabbed five more boxes of ammo, and they ran out of the apartment. Jinx was a hell of a driver and knew the city almost as well as Harbinger did. Except ... "No, turn here. It'll cut five minutes."

Jinx made the corner—barely. They screamed through the narrow streets, and Jinx pulled into a dark lot and parked the car.

Ranger was on the horn and setting up his

people and the people of Delta Team. "This way." Jinx led him through a maze of alleyways to where they could see the warehouse in the distance.

"Ranger, we'll need a distraction to pull eyes off the back of the warehouse."

"I've got that," Giovanni answered. "Give me three minutes."

Harbinger and Jinx remained in the darkened alleyway until they heard a vehicle approach. "Hold," Con said. "Well, shit."

"What?" Harbinger hissed.

"Giovanni. She's wearing next to nothing, and yeah, nobody is going to be looking at you … go!"

Harbinger and Jinx moved. Shadow to shadow, they moved quickly and silently. Jinx stopped, pointed at the fence line to the back of the warehouse, and signed. "Watch and copy."

Harbinger nodded. Jinx moved to the fence, and … Holy hell, the guy opened a section of fence and slipped in. The fence swung back and looked complete once again.

"Go," Jinx whispered.

He hustled after Jinx, found the panel, and slipped into the compound. He closed the fence soundlessly and turned, frozen to the spot. If there ever was an ass-puckering moment, that was it.

Three Dobermans, teeth bared, stood growling at him. Jinx snapped his fingers, and all three dogs turned and hustled to him. He leaned down and loved on each of them for a moment before motioning for Harbinger to come forward.

The dogs barely gave him a sideways glance. Jinx motioned, and Harbinger followed the man and his canine escorts.

"Giovanni, you've got three vehicles incoming." That was Jewell's voice.

"Merci beaucoup," she said sweetly, and Harbinger could hear what sounded like a hood closing. Giovanni cooed in French, "It worked! You're an angel." A few seconds later, she said in English. "I'm clear, heading back to my position."

"Roger. Those vehicles are pulling up at the front of the building," Jewell said.

Jinx moved, and Harbinger followed. That was the distraction they'd needed. Jinx went first, and Harbinger followed, the dogs' asses planted where Jinx told them to stay.

As they slipped into the building, he heard Con's voice in his ear. "I'm looping each camera as you move. Stop when I tell you. Where do you want to be set up?"

"As close as we can get without being compromised."

"Down the hall, you're clear."

The men hustled down the tiled passage.

"Holy shit!" Jewell's exclamation froze both Harbinger and Jinx. "That's Abrasha."

Harbinger's comm device fell silent. He knew Archangel and the executive team were hashing things out.

Harbinger growled, "Con, get us closer."

"Hold on, if you move, you and the newcomers are going to collide."

Ranger came online. "Con, both teams in position and holding."

"Copy. Okay, H, go forward, and at the end of the hall, turn left. Enter the fourth door on the right. That's the men's bathroom and the closest I can get you to the epicenter. It's literally ten feet away."

Harbinger and Jinx moved rapidly and into the bathroom. Jinx cleared the stalls, and Harbinger opened the door a fraction. "The double doors?"

"Yep," Con replied.

"H and Jinx, the goal now is to take Abrasha and Pierre, but only after the crypto is moved." Archangel gave them their orders.

"Abrasha is wanted. We can take him now," Fury hissed.

"I'm aware, but if we want a solid conviction, we wait. The Rostova incident isn't ironclad because most of the participants are dead and those who're willing to testify are dying at an alarming pace. We're recording him, with Pierre, stealing billions. Iron clad. And with Nadia and Pierre in custody, we can leverage more charges against him." Archangel's explanation made sense.

"Con, they've already unlocked most of the passwords on all of these accounts." Jewell sounded worried.

"They must've had the chain when we saw them this morning. They're really close to opening all of them."

"Can we listen to what's happening in that room?" Archangel asked.

"Maybe. Hold on," Con said.

"No mics on the computers," Jewell interjected.

"Phones?" Con then laughed. "Archambeau has the cloned phone on him. I don't know how clear it will be, but I can activate the mic on his phone."

"Do it," Archangel commanded.

"Nothing," Jewell said.

"They aren't talking, or we aren't receiving?" Fury wanted clarification.

"We're receiving," Con answered.

"Con," Jewell commanded.

"I see it. We're going to get real busy in five …"

"Four, three, two, and the transfer has started. Where are you going?" Jewell asked no one in particular.

"Got it. I'm working on getting in." Con sounded stressed.

Harbinger kept an eye on the double doors. They'd move soon. He wanted both of those bastards in his sights. He looked back at Jinx. "Get ready." They both put silencers on their weapons. "The guards first. If we can keep it quiet, we might be able to avoid a war outside."

"What fun is that?" Ranger joked. "But we're outnumbered; although we have higher ground … for the most part."

"We're in."

"Hold until it all goes." Archangel's voice was steady and certain.

"Four more transfers."

The seconds ticked through frozen molasses, each one seeming to take a minute. Harbinger's adrenaline was spiked. "I'll take everything to the right in the room. You take everything to the left."

"Abrasha's description?" Jinx asked.

"Tall, brown hair, the only one wearing a suit." That was Fury's voice. "Pierre and Abrasha are watching the transfer on a large video screen at the back of the room. Seven guards and five computer techs between you and them. Abrasha has two personal bodyguards flanking him."

"Entrances and exits?" Harbinger wanted to know where help or trouble would come from.

"Double doors at both ends of the room."

"Don't exit the building on a chase. We're taking out anything that comes out of a door," Ranger replied.

"Noted," Harbinger confirmed.

"Hold … And that's it."

A huge cheer could be heard from the operators. "Go!" Fury commanded, and Harbinger and Jinx moved as one.

CHAPTER 21

Harbinger and Jinx slammed through the doors, catching the room by surprise. The guards, however, were good and dropped into covered positions that had to be predetermined. Harbinger was able to down two of the four on the right side before return fire started. He trusted Jinx to take care of his people. Harbinger lifted and pulled the trigger on one of Abrasha's bodyguards, dropping him. He rolled back and moved, lifting just in time to see Abrasha shoot Pierre. The remaining bodyguard pulled Abrasha toward the back doors. Harbinger ran toward the back of the room, firing as he moved. Jinx was right with him.

The sprinting attack caused bullets to miss, and

Harbinger hit both of his guards; although he couldn't confirm they were kill shots. They both barreled out the door after Abrasha. They hit the deck as suppression fire hit the door. The guard gave Abrasha time to get out. Fuck.

Harbinger glanced at Jinx. They had minimal cover. He signed, "Rolling out, you take him."

Jinx narrowed his eyes but nodded. Harbinger counted down and rolled out, his gun trained down the hall. There was no firing. He was on his feet, following Jinx down the hall. They skidded to a stop at the exit. The guard lay half in, half out the door, dead. "I'll wait for the all clear here." Jinx pulled the man into the building as Harbinger hustled back to the room where the computer techs were still hiding under their desks. One of the guards who'd been injured opened fire. Harbinger dove to the floor, rolled, and fired. The man went down, and that time, he wouldn't get up.

Harbinger moved from guard to guard, making sure they weren't going to be an issue. As he moved past the computer techs, he growled. "If you move from where you are, you're dead."

He could hear the gunfight continuing outside. The distinct sound of two marksman rifles told him the high ground was the right place to be. He kept his back to both doors and made his way to Pierre.

The man had a chest wound but barely any blood on his shirt. Harbinger ripped open the man's shirt. The swell of the abdomen was an indication of internal bleeding and a lot of it. Pierre grabbed his arm and tried to talk. Harbinger leaned down.

"Abrasha shot me."

"I know. I'm sorry I wasn't the one to kill you, you fucking bastard."

Pierre coughed. "She gets nothing."

"That's where you're wrong. She gets me." Harbinger stood and glared at the dying man.

"Pierre is dying," he said into the comms because they were suddenly silent.

"Abrasha is gone." Ranger sighed. "I have two injured, but not serious. The body count for the others is unknown."

"Everyone get out. CCS, block all cameras for the exit. French police are en route."

"Computer techs?"

"Leave them," Archangel said. "CCS, fry their equipment."

"Including the supercomputer?" Jewell asked.

"Spike it," Archangel confirmed.

"Roger," Con said. "Cameras are all out. I didn't have time to pick and choose. Exit now."

Jinx ran back into the room, and they jogged out together, back the way they'd come. As they exited the fenced area, Jinx whistled for the dogs, and they followed them through the alleyways to the car. Jinx opened the back door, and the dogs hopped in and sat down.

Harbinger glanced back at the animals. "Spike isn't going to like them in his space."

Jinx chuckled. "I agree, but I couldn't leave them there. They're not being cared for properly."

And that summed up Jinx. He was a hell of an assassin, and Harbinger would take him as a wingman any day, but he liked animals better than he did people. Hell, Harbinger leaned back against the headrest and figured animals were more trustworthy than most people. The guy had a point.

He sighed. He was glad he hadn't killed Pierre. Living with the knowledge he'd killed his soon-to-be wife's father would be a heavy weight to bear. But he wasn't lying to the bastard. He did want to be the one to do it. Conflicting emotions and thoughts, to be sure. Maybe someday they'd resolve, but he wouldn't waste a second worrying about the man or his death.

On the trip back to his apartment, which was now home base to the teams and Jinx, they listened to the techies as they worked. The barrage of French police cars that passed them was impressive.

Jinx pulled over at an all-night market and went inside. "Food for them and us."

Harbinger looked back at the Dobies. They sat perfectly still, staring after the man who'd rescued them.

Fury's voice came over his comms. "H, we need to do a debrief. What's your ETA?"

"We had to make a stop. We'll be there shortly."

"Status?"

"Secure. But we've got three hungry Dobermans in the car, and I don't want them to eat my cat."

There was silence on the line. "Jinx," Fury finally said.

"It was me. Yes," Jinx replied.

"Can you *not* go on a mission without picking up a stray?" Fury asked in a particularly sarcastic voice.

"I don't see where acquiring stray animals is against my terms of employment. If I'm wrong, please advise as to what you'd like me to do with the animals. They're not at fault."

Harbinger chuckled as he watched Jinx walk out of the market loaded with bags.

"Just get back to the apartment," Fury growled, and the line went quiet again.

Once Jinx put the bags in the trunk, they returned to the apartment.

* * *

HARBINGER WAS CORRECT. Spike was not a fan. The dogs were well-trained and didn't budge when the cat hissed and bowed up. They sat where they were told and watched Spike's antics. Jinx fed the animals quickly, and he, Ranger, and Jinx went into the comm room.

"We're online," Con said and then gave each person's call sign as the meeting started.

"What happened to Abrasha?" Harbinger asked.

"His people protected him with their lives. The vehicles he arrived in were armored," Ranger answered.

"Other factions in CCS tracked him to an airstrip. He's heading to Russia."

"And the money?" Jinx asked.

"Oh, dude, that is safe." Con chuckled.

"Your people, Ranger, are they in need of a doctor?"

"Nah, my medic has it. Are we to bring home Delta team, too?"

"Yes, we have two teams heading to Europe in the morning. The plane will refuel and come down to get all of you," Jacob answered.

"Do we have enough to go after Abrasha?" Harbinger wanted the bastard. If he couldn't take out Pierre, he wanted a shot at the person who pulled his strings.

"That decision will be made at a later time," Fury answered, knowing he wasn't talking about an arrest. No one else in the room, excluding Jinx, would know either.

"It was good work tonight and leading up to this event. We'll let Con know when the aircraft will land. Bring it home."

"Copy," Harbinger said and listened as everyone cleared.

"Gentlemen, I have a healthy bar that will be abandoned. Let's not leave it for my housekeeper." Harbinger glanced at Con. "You, too. You did well tonight."

Con stretched and nodded at his computer. "I

have a few things left. I'll be out shortly." Jinx and Ranger headed out to take him up on his offer.

Harbinger cocked his head. "What's up?"

"I haven't been this close to a big mission before." Con frowned. "I mean, I showed up after Ice went all assassin on that island, and the explosion was impressive, but I was in a computer room away from everything." Con rubbed the back of his neck. "Dude, how many people died tonight and today?"

Harbinger crossed his arms over his chest. "None who didn't absolutely need to die. We didn't initiate the firefight. These men were professionals. They traded their lives for money and aligned themselves with evil people. What happened tonight wasn't because you were close to a mission. What happened tonight was because the world contains evil people who do evil things. We're here to ensure they don't prey on society or hurt the innocent. What happened here tonight was a fashion of justice that most people never know about."

Con nodded. "I get that. It's tough, though. Behind a keyboard thousands of miles away from where the leather meets the ground, it's different."

"The wizard behind the curtain type of thing?"

"Yeah, exactly." Con snorted.

"Most of us don't have that privilege. If you need to talk to someone, I can recommend a professional."

"I'm all right, or I will be. It drives home the fact that this isn't just keystrokes. Lives are at stake."

Harbinger nodded. "Hard lesson."

Con sighed, agreeing, "Extremely."

"Come have a drink. This can wait."

Con looked at the computer and turned off the screen. "Sounds like a plan."

CHAPTER 22

Val took Harbinger's go-bag with his weapons, IDs, and cash from his hand and pointed down the hallway to the left, saying, "Second room on the right. I'll store this in my vault. And give him some milk and a bit of chopped chicken." She pointed at the carrier at his feet. Spike was glaring at him as if he were Satan incarnate. To say he was not happy to be crated was an understatement.

"Thanks, you didn't tell her?" Harbinger asked.

"I figured a surprise would be better." Val winked. "I'm taking Smith to a follow-up appointment, so the house is yours for the next three hours or so. Give me ten minutes to secure this, feed Spike, and get my husband rounded up."

"Thanks, Val. For everything." Harbinger pulled her in for a hug.

"Whatever it takes, my brother by another mother." She laughed as she pulled away. "And I do consider you a brother. No more keeping us at arm's length."

"I'll do better, and I love you, too." Harbinger raised his hand when her eyebrows hit her hairline. "In a completely appropriate brother-sister-I'd-rather-pull-your-ponytail-and-run-away kind of way."

"Thank goodness." She laughed and smacked him on the arm. "Go tell your woman you're here."

Harbinger winked at her and went to find Ysabel. He opened the door quietly and stepped in. Ysabel came out of the bathroom, wrapped in a towel and drying her hair. She startled when she saw him. The shock lasted a total of two seconds before she ran toward him. Catching her in his arms, he pulled her into a hug. Her arms wrapped around him, and the towel lost its anchor, fluttering to the floor at her feet. "Why didn't you tell me you were on your way back?"

He didn't answer. Instead, he kissed her neck, moved to her ear, and then to her lips. Their tongues danced as his hands slid down the smooth expanse of her back to her waist. His hand moved lower, around her firm bottom, and lifted her leg to his hip. God, he wanted her. Ysabel's hands slipped between them, and she somehow unfastened his slacks and freed his cock.

He pulled his lips away long enough to say, "Bed."

She shook her head and made a noise. He chased her lips when she pulled away and panted, "Like this." She jumped a bit, and he caught her other leg. Her hand slid between them again, and she helped him find home.

When he slid into her, she gasped. He froze. "Are you okay?"

"More." She grabbed his cheeks and pulled him to her for a kiss. Harbinger didn't need to be told twice. He lifted her and slid her back down his shaft. The sensation of her sliding over his cock in that position was insane. He shifted, widening his stance, and, holding her up by her thighs, he lifted her again. God, he wouldn't last. Each thrust brought them closer to that perfect moment of unmatched release. When it came to Ysabel, he was insatiable. He would have to apologize to her. He wasn't going to last. He wasn't going to ... Her legs tightened around him, and she clenched, which pulled the trigger on his orgasm. Her groan and his combined as they fell into nothing but sensation and release. He held her against him and prayed he'd be able to keep them upright.

Her head lulled on his shoulder, and she kissed his neck. "You're back."

He chuffed out a laugh. "Best welcome ever." After carefully withdrawing, he put her down.

She took his hand. "Bed, now." She helped him undress, and they fell into bed together. He pulled her into him and flipped the sheets over their cooling skin. Nestled together, he sighed heavily. She looked up at him. "What's wrong?"

"I lost my mind for a minute there. I wanted to tell you something before we made love."

She moved and propped her head up on her hand. "What?"

"It's about your father." He pushed her damp hair away from her face.

"He's dead," she said with a slight hesitation in her voice. Her eyes misted, and she stared at him intently. Harbinger could see the immense sadness in her eyes. "The French police called my phone." A tear formed in the corner of her eye. "They said it looked like a robbery gone bad. There were people who were working there with my father that night.

One of them saw a man shoot my father when the attack started. They believe the people chasing the man who killed my father weren't after my dad or anyone working. He was in the wrong place at the wrong time. You were one of the people chasing the man who shot my father, weren't you?"

He nodded. "I was there. I saw the man who killed him, and we chased after him, but he got away. I talked to your father before he died. He was thinking of you." Which wasn't a lie, and maybe it would comfort her in some way. Her eyes welled with tears, and she shook her head. Harbinger pulled her down onto his arm. He brushed her hair back behind her ear. "Are you okay?"

"I'm trying to be. I think I'm still in shock from everything that happened in France. I know my father wasn't a good man. Still …" She sighed and closed her eyes. When she opened them, she changed the subject. "What happened to Nadia?"

"She was brought back to the States and will be questioned for her part in several crimes. Con finished scanning all those documents before we headed back. Your mom's evidence is vast. Guardian will be able to use it to prosecute Nadia."

"And Abrasha?" Ysabel asked.

"I haven't been briefed on anything regarding him, and I probably won't be unless it becomes my assignment to work." Which, unfortunately, was the truth. He would make sure his handlers knew he wanted that folio.

"No work now, though, right?"

He smiled. "No work now. Do you want to go back to France for his funeral?"

"No. I called his lawyer, who said everything was taken care of via my father's will and instructions. We're starting over. Here. A wedding, a house, a new job for me."

"We are." Harbinger lifted up and rolled her onto her back, hovering over her. "How about I make up for the lack of foreplay just now?"

Ysabel laughed and framed his face with her hands. "But I don't have any lace on."

He growled and descended on her, attacking her throat with kisses. "All the better."

EPILOGUE

 *welve hours earlier:*

CON FINISHED UPLOADING the documents to CCS and shut down his computer. He placed the flat and the two trackers into a portable Faraday case for the flight back to America. He didn't want anything to compromise the original source of the material he processed and sent back to the States. He'd stopped looking at the documents and just scanned and sent. The sheer volume of information was astounding. The plane would be landing in an hour, and he had just enough time to pack up before the entire contingent would load up and leave. Dogs, cat, and all.

His phone rang, and he glanced down at the screen. He closed his eyes and counted to ten before answering. "Hi, Mom. I'm kind of busy."

"Oh, dear, sorry to hear that." Olivia Solomon sounded anything but sorry. "I'm calling in one of those chips, dear. There's a ball in Monaco I need you to attend on behalf of the family."

"I don't know if I can get the time."

"Do I need to call my contacts in Guardian?"

Con could see his mother's eyebrows raise in his mind. "I'm a big boy. I can ask for time off."

"Good. I'll send you a copy of the invitation via email. Your older brother was going to attend, but the merger he's working on is coming to a head."

"Wait, when is this event?"

"Saturday night."

"This Saturday?" Con's shout brought Harbinger into the bedroom. He held up a finger to the assassin.

"Will that be a problem? I'll have Darren book you a flight."

"I'm in France."

"Oh, well, all the better. Darren can book you a flight from there. I'll have him call you to figure out the details. Thanks for this, darling."

He started to say something but realized his

mother had already hung up. Con turned to Harbinger. "Can I use your apartment until Friday?"

"Sure. You're not going back to the States with us?"

"It would seem not. I need to attend a family function this weekend. Working from here would be easier. I'll pop over to Monaco for the weekend and then head home on a commercial flight on Monday."

Harbinger frowned at him. "Your family has functions in Monaco?"

Con snickered. "My family has functions everywhere." He handed Harbinger the small Faraday case. "The flat and the trackers. Maybe our forensic people can determine where the trackers came from and why the phones appear to be manufactured with trackers. Man, this entire mission was nothing but crossed wires. Abrasha may or may not have killed his wife, but we do know she's dead. But his dead wife already sent Ysabel the ring in the envelope. A fake funeral, arranged by Ysabel's dead mom, is where a messenger delivers the envelope to Ysabel. Meanwhile, Pierre is working with Abrasha and screwing him on the side with Abrasha's own daughter. Pierre arranges the kidnapping of Ysabel from Corsica or at least has knowledge of it. And after all that conniving, Pierre still gets gut shot by Abrasha."

"Abrasha is a bloodthirsty mother fucker. Remember, he wasn't the only one who wanted Pierre dead. I wanted to shoot Pierre. I couldn't imagine Abrasha cared for Pierre's manipulations any more than I did. We'll get more answers, but not tonight." Harbinger took the case. "I have to go load Spike into a carrier. It isn't going to be easy."

"Have Jinx do it," Con called after him. Jinx was a savant with animals.

Con dropped his head. He didn't want to go to Monaco. He wanted to continue the search for the assassin he'd met on that island. Oh, he was stealthy while poking around Guardian's systems, but there was nothing about her. Nothing, which was the norm for the assassins. Nothing on that beautiful woman. "My name's Centurion, but you can call me Ronnie." Con could hear her voice in his thoughts. She had a smoking hot body, and he liked everything about the woman. She was intelligent, articulate, and jumped out of airplanes. The thrill of that high-altitude jump still coursed through his veins, and he couldn't find out anything about her. He could ask, but … If she was married and had a family, he didn't want anyone to know he had a thing for her. That would be something he'd never live down. Fury would make sure of it. Yeah, so not a damn thing to go on, and that was a challenge he wasn't going to let go of.

He looked at his phone and pushed the number for his supervisor. "Hey, Jewell. Got a minute? I need to take this weekend off. Can that be arranged?"

WANT to read Con's and Centurion's story? Click here.

ALSO BY KRIS MICHAELS

Kings of the Guardian Series

Jacob: Kings of the Guardian Book 1

Joseph: Kings of the Guardian Book 2

Adam: Kings of the Guardian Book 3

Jason: Kings of the Guardian Book 4

Jared: Kings of the Guardian Book 5

Jasmine: Kings of the Guardian Book 6

Chief: The Kings of Guardian Book 7

Jewell: Kings of the Guardian Book 8

Jade: Kings of the Guardian Book 9

Justin: Kings of the Guardian Book 10

Christmas with the Kings

Drake: Kings of the Guardian Book 11

Dixon: Kings of the Guardian Book 12

Passages: The Kings of Guardian Book 13

Promises: The Kings of Guardian Book 14

The Siege: Book One, The Kings of Guardian Book 15

The Siege: Book Two, The Kings of Guardian Book 16

A Backwater Blessing: A Kings of Guardian Crossover Novella

Montana Guardian: A Kings of Guardian Novella

Guardian Defenders Series

Gabriel

Maliki

John

Jeremiah

Frank

Creed

Sage

Bear

Billy

Elliot

Guardian Security Shadow World

Anubis (Guardian Shadow World Book 1)

Asp (Guardian Shadow World Book 2)

Lycos (Guardian Shadow World Book 3)

Thanatos (Guardian Shadow World Book 4)

Tempest (Guardian Shadow World Book 5)

Smoke (Guardian Shadow World Book 6)

Reaper (Guardian Shadow World Book 7)

Phoenix (Guardian Shadow World Book 8)

Valkyrie (Guardian Shadow World Book 9)

Flack (Guardian Shadow World Book 10)

Ice (Guardian Shadow World Book 11)

Malice (Guardian Shadow World Book 12)

Harbinger (Guardian Shadow World Book 13)

Centurion (Guardian Shadow World Book 14)

Hollister (A Guardian Crossover Series)

Andrew (Hollister-Book 1)

Zeke (Hollister-Book 2)

Declan (Hollister- Book 3)

Ken (Hollister - Book 4)

Barry (Hollister - Book 5)

Hope City

Hope City - Brock

HOPE CITY - Brody- Book 3

Hope City - Ryker - Book 5

Hope City - Killian - Book 8

Hope City - Blayze - Book 10

The Long Road Home

Season One:

My Heart's Home

Season Two:

Searching for Home (A Hollister-Guardian Crossover Novel)

Season Three:

A Home for Love (A Hollister Crossover Novel)

Season Four:

Finally Home

STAND-ALONE NOVELS

A Heart's Desire - Stand Alone

Hot SEAL, Single Malt (SEALs in Paradise)

Hot SEAL, Savannah Nights (SEALs in Paradise)

Hot SEAL, Silent Knight (SEALs in Paradise)

Join my newsletter for fun updates and release information!

>>>Kris' Newsletter<<<

ABOUT THE AUTHOR

Wall Street Journal and USA Today Bestselling Author, Kris Michaels is the alter ego of a happily married wife and mother. She writes romance, usually with characters from military and law enforcement backgrounds.

Made in the USA
Coppell, TX
01 May 2024